The Stones of Courage

BOOK TWO OF THE CENTAUR CHRONICLES

M.J. Evans

Dancing Horse Press

Foxfield, Colorado

The Centaur Chronicles

Book 2

The Stone of Courage

M.J.Evans

M.J. Evans/Dancing Horse Press

7013 S. Telluride St.

Foxfield, CO 80016

www.dancinghorsepress.com

Book Layout ©2017 BookDesignTemplates.com

Ordering Information:

Quantity sales. Special discounts are available on quantity purchases by corporations, associations, and others. For details, contact the "Special Sales Department" at the address above.

The Stone of Mercy/ M.J. Evans. —1st ed.

ISBN 978-1-946229-71-7

Contents

*This book is dedicated to all those children,
young and old,
who have the courage to choose the right
even when it's hard!*

*"Stand therefore,
having your loins girt about with truth,
and having on the breastplate of
righteousness."*

Eph. 6:14 (KJV)

CHAPTER 1

Training a Queen

SOMETHING INSIDE TOLD CARLING that a change was coming. She couldn't explain it, but she could feel it. And it wasn't something she was welcoming.

Carling had been up for several hours, gazing out the small round window in her room over the village bakery. The stars faded as, softly and gently, the sun unfurled its splendor across the face of Mount Dashmore, the western hogback and, finally, the little valley that protected the village of Duenton. Spring was making its presence known all across the country known as Crystonia. The lush valley in which the village of Duenton nestled was emerging from the heavy white winter blanket that had covered it for several months. Fresh green sprigs of grass and tiny leaves were making their appearance.

She fidgeted as she looked out the window, the muscles in her neck twitching. It was not the change of seasons that was making her so restive.

Carling, a member of the little Duende race that populated the land of Crystonia, left the window and walked across her room. She could smell the aroma of freshly baked bread wafting up from the kitchen below. It made her smile. Something about the smell of bread always made her feel contented. It brought back happy memories of her childhood. She sighed, well aware that, at just seventeen, her childhood was forever lost to her.

She approached the Silver Breastplate with its large, sparkling, green Stone of Mercy nestled in one of four holes arranged on the front. It was sitting on a chair beside her bed. She ran her fingertips over the intricate carved designs that had been worked into the silver. The young Duende thought of the heavy responsibility that was now hers because she had been given the breastplate by the Wizard of Crystonia. The one green stone, the first of the four Stones of Light that she must gather to complete her mission, provided only a small glimmer of hope and encouragement. Carling pulled off her nightgown and picked up the armor. Placing it over her body and latching it on the side, she quickly covered it with a rough tunic.

She glanced in the mirror on the wall beside her bed. Frowning, Carling paused long enough to run a brush through her unruly auburn curls. Her violet eyes squinted as she examined the outcome of her halfhearted effort. The results of the brushing weren't very good, but she didn't have time to work harder on her appearance. *It doesn't matter anyway*, she told herself as she tucked an errant strand of hair behind her pointed ear, an inheritance from the fairies through which all Duende were descended.

She hurried down the back stairs and entered the bakery's kitchen. "I have some sweet rolls cooling on the table. Help yourself," offered Parkson, the baker.

Carling stepped up to the little Duende. He was shorter than her, and a lifetime of sampling breads had left him much plumper as well. She gave him a hug, an expression of the genuine affection she had for this man and his family. They had taken her in several months before when her parents had been killed by a band of marauding Centaurs who had destroyed their village. "Thank you, Parkson. What would I do without you to take care of me?"

"You'd probably die," he said with a twinkle in his eye.

Whether Parkson was joking or not, Carling realized he was probably right. This little Duende family of bakers had sheltered her while she was directing the building of the wall around the village of Duenton. After the completion of the barrier, they insisted that she remain with them, sensitive to the fact that the loss of her parents at the hands of the Heilodius Centaurs had left her homeless and orphaned.

Carling helped herself to a roll, some bottled peaches, and a glass of milk. She sat down to eat her breakfast. As she did so, she watched the baker knead some bread dough. His pushes and pulls sent flour flying around him to settle in his hair and stick to his face and arms. He was getting whiter by the minute and the sight made Carling smile.

When she was done eating, Carling cleaned her dishes and then stepped up beside Parkson to help him cut the dough into rolls. He said nothing, but the smile on his face told Carling that he appreciated her help.

Once the last of the rolls were in the oven, Carling gave Parkson another hug. He blushed and brushed his flour-covered hands over his face, leaving a fresh smear of white. "Go on, you silly girl," he said. "You have more important things to do than help an old man bake bread."

Carling dashed out the door of the bakery. She was intent on finding her best friend, Higson. The wall Carling had convinced the village to build had done its job in protecting those inside the barrier when the Heilodius Herd of Centaurs attacked for the second time. But Higson's parents had refused to leave their cottage nestled in the forest outside the wall. Now Higson was an orphan as well.

It had taken time, but Carling was finally feeling that Higson no longer blamed her for the loss of his parents. It had been a struggle. It seemed to Carling that the shared experience of losing their parents should have brought them closer together. The death of their parents had cut them both open, making them bleed and leaving them both scarred and scared.

But instead of turning to Carling for comfort, Higson seemed to prefer to suffer alone. The pain and fear Carling felt at the thought of losing her friendship with Higson was more than she could bear. She was relieved that he was finally stronger emotionally and had healed enough to return to being her steady and constant companion.

"Higson, are you there?" she asked as she entered the small park on the east end of the village within the safety of the walls. The twang from a bow and arrow answered her question. Higson stood in the center of the park, shooting at a target. His arrows all hit their mark. They always did. He turned and smiled at Carling as she approached.

The sight of him warmed her heart. The two of them had been born on the same day, grown up together, and—except for the few months after the loss of his parents—had always been the best of friends.

Carling was a good head taller than her friend. She was also much slimmer and stunningly beautiful. Higson's angular face, framed by short, wavy, brown hair, though not terribly handsome, reflected the goodness within him. His body, at three feet tall, average for a Duende, was strong. His skin was rough from a life spent outdoors hunting and cutting wood. Even after the death of his parents, he had continued to work as a hunter, bringing fresh meats and cut wood to the village markets.

Higson lowered his bow and rubbed the stubble on his chin, a sign that, at seventeen, he was maturing into a man. The past year had aged them, and they had both lost their childish features as completely as they had lost their childhood dreams.

"What are we going to work on today?" Carling asked. The two Duende had been working on their battle skills, knowing they would have to face not only the Heilodius Centaurs but probably the Ogres and Cyclops as well. The three larger races were in constant strife over the control of the throne high atop Mount Heilodius. As the bearer of the Silver Breastplate, Carling was the rightful heir to the throne, but that didn't mean securing it would be easy.

Both Carling and Higson were adept at the bow and arrow. However, having watched a gruesome battle between the Heilodius Centaurs and a band of Cyclops, they realized they needed to expand their abilities with more weapons.

"We're going to learn to fight with a sword," Higson replied. The young Duende walked over to two swords he had previously placed on the ground. He bent down and picked them up. "Choose your weapon, my dear," he said, extending both his arms.

Carling shrugged, knowing nothing about swords. She took the one from his left hand. "How are you going to teach me about swords? What do you know about them?"

"Nothing. Or at least *almost* nothing. I'm not going to be the teacher." He looked over her shoulder and Carling turned to follow his gaze. An old Duende man was entering the park.

"Ashtic! I didn't know you were a swordsman," Carling said. Ashtic was the highly-respected blacksmith of the village. Everyone knew him to be the very best at his craft. It was Ashtic who had crafted the Silver Breastplate under the direction of the Wizard of Crystonia. Carling knew this, but she had no idea he was proficient with the sword.

"All my life, my dear," he said, bowing deeply. "Now, let's get to work. You have a lot to learn, both of you." He handed each of them a stick and they set their swords down on the ground. The smithy was older than Higson's and Carling's parents had been when they died, old enough, in fact, to be Higson's or Carling's grandfather. But a life of hard work had kept him strong despite the frequent cough he'd developed from constantly breathing in the smoke in his shop. He coughed now and wiped his forehead with a handkerchief. Then he pushed his dark hair back from his eyes and lowered his single dark eyebrow.

Stepping back, he began demonstrating various positions and techniques to be used when fighting with a sword. Ashtic swung his stick overhead, sideways, underhanded, showing them every way they might need to swing a sword. Carling and Higson did their best to mimic the moves Ashtic was teaching them. Their sticks clashed against one another as they were taught how to block and dodge.

Carling had the advantage of height. At three and a half feet tall, she was the tallest Duende in the village and a good six inches taller than Higson. But Higson had the advantage of strength. They spun and twirled and did their best to follow Ashtic's directives. The sticks cracked and splintered under the force of their swings. Not until Ashtic felt they could handle a sword well enough to avoid slicing each other up did he let them pick up the real weapons.

Already tired, Carling bent down and clasped the handle of her sword. She tried swinging it around as she had done with the stick. It felt slow and heavy in comparison. Discouraged, she dropped her hand to her side, letting the tip of the sword pierce the ground. "Maybe I'm not cut out for this," she said with a sigh.

Ashtic stepped up to her and looked into her violet eyes. With his finger, he tapped her chest, hitting the shield, the shield he had made. "I'm afraid you have no choice, my dear," he said sympathetically.

Carling shrugged, took a deep breath, and lifted her sword.

Over the course of the next two weeks, Carling could tell both she and Higson were improving in their ability to fight with a sword. While still happier with a bow and arrow, Carling admitted she was beginning to feel more confident with this new weapon. Her arm was getting stronger and her reflexes were getting quicker.

On one occasion when she got tired, she tried to counter balance the weight of the sword by extending her other arm. This was met with a hard whack from Ashtic. "Keep your arms in or you'll lose one of them," Ashtic shouted at her. She glared at him, rubbing the bruise that rapidly appeared on her forearm. But Carling kept going. Something told her these would be skills she would need as she continued her quest to complete the Silver Breastplate and gather the three remaining Stones of Light.

"Keep your knees bent. Never turn your back on your enemy. Try to figure out what they are thinking before they think it!" Ashtic grilled them relentlessly.

Tibbals and Tandum, Carling's and Higson's Centaur friends, joined in the training whenever possible. It seemed to Carling that the brother and sister caught on to the use of the sword much more quickly than the Duende. As a species, the Centaurs were much stronger and much quicker. They had four legs that enabled them to spin around swiftly and reposition themselves. In addition, they could rear up on their hind legs, a practice Ashtic cautioned them against. "You're exposing your vital organs to a shorter foe. Only do that maneuver if you are fighting something as tall as you are."

Steadily, under the watchful eye and careful instruction provided by Ashtic, all four friends improved.

Ashtic wasn't able to be with them all the time. He had a business to run. Instead, he came each day, taught them some new technique, then left to attend to his work in his blacksmith shop, leaving his protégés to practice on their own. The method seemed to be working quite well.

After several hours of sparring with Higson, Tibbals, and Tandum, Carling always returned to her little room over the bakery both sore and tired. She collapsed on her bed, too tired to eat, and fell into a restless sleep. In her dreams, she searched throughout the land for the remaining stones to complete the Silver Breastplate. But in none of her dreams did she see herself as a righteous queen.

CHAPTER 2

The Wizard Returns

IT WAS ON A blustery cold day during a late spring storm when the trees were whipping against one another and most of the Duende were hiding in their homes that the anticipated, yet dreaded, change came.

Carling and Higson were outside the walls of the village, roaming through the brush and tree-covered hills that surrounded the village of Duenton. Both of them were wrapped in several layers of clothing to shield them from the cold and blowing snow. They were hunting for any animal they could bring back to cook in the baker's oven. Not having any luck, they decided to separate. Carling's senses were on high alert as she was fully aware the forest could be a dangerous place. She wished Tibbals or Tandum were with her.

Stepping softly around a tree, Carling stopped. Her experienced eyes scanned the flattened snow. A family of deer had bedded down here during the night. She looked for their prints in the snow-covered ground and began following their tracks. As stealthily as a cat, she wound through the forest until she came upon a forest glen. In the gray and white meadow, deer in a small herd were pawing through the snow, attempting to find some new spring grass. Without making a sound, she slid an arrow out of her quiver, nocked it on the bow string, raised her elbow, and started to pull back.

Just as she set her aim for the closest deer, the creature's head jerked up and turned away from Carling, staring toward the far side of the glen. Instantly in quick, bouncing leaps, the deer at which she was aiming, along with the entire herd, turned and darted straight toward her. Carling lowered her bow and slipped behind a large tree just as the deer crashed through the underbrush and ran past, sending sprays of snow all over her.

Carling heard shouts coming from the meadow and peeked around the tree. Her heart leaped to her throat and her face turned ashen as she saw a band of Heilodius Centaurs charge into the field. She recognized them immediately from the black and silver tunics they wore over their strong torsos. This was the herd that had split off from the Minsheen herd to which Tibbals and Tandum belonged. This was the herd that had destroyed her village and killed her parents. They were armed with bows and arrows, their weapon of choice, and were galloping straight toward her, the scarves tied around their necks flapping in the wind.

Not knowing if this was a hunting party or a war party, Carling turned and ran in the direction of her village. Gripping her bow, she pumped her well-muscled arms as she slipped and slid in the snow. Her beating heart matched the pounding of her dainty feet on the forest floor. She jumped over fallen logs and snow-filled ditches. But as fast as she was, it wasn't fast enough. She heard the Centaurs' hooves crashing through the forest vegetation. The young girl could tell they were getting closer to her. She could hear their panting. Carling could almost feel the ground shaking beneath her, though she wasn't sure if the shaking was from the Centaurs or her own trembling body.

Carling realized she was losing this race and her best option was to find a place to hide. She hoped they had not yet spotted her. Her eyes darted to her left, and she noticed a dark opening in the side of an enormous sandstone rock that was nearly concealed by fallen branches. Carling dashed to the side, jumped over some leafless, snow-covered bushes and dove into the black entrance to the cave. Crouching down, she pressed her back against the stone wall and hugged her knees. Beads of sweat formed on her upper lip and forehead. She held her breath and stared out the opening of the cave as the snow began falling like a fluttering curtain, helping to conceal her.

She didn't have to wait long before she heard the Centaurs galloping through the forest just in front of the cave. They didn't stop or slow down. Clearly, they had not seen her through the falling snow. Now her thoughts jumped to Higson and her village. Higson, the great woodsman that he was, would certainly hear the Centaurs coming and conceal himself. But if the Centaurs were headed to the village, intent on launching another attack, would the Fauns on the village watchtowers spot them coming through the falling snow before they got too close? The Fauns that Carling had rescued from enslavement to the Cyclops were now in charge of helping to guard her village, and they took their job seriously. But even so, Carling wondered if they would have time to secure the city gates. She said a silent prayer that the Fauns would see or hear the Centaurs coming soon enough to do so. Of course, she wasn't even sure the Centaurs were going to the village. Perhaps she was worrying for no purpose.

Carling crawled forward on her hands and knees and peeked around the edge of the cave. Holding her breath, she listened. As soon as she was sure all the Heilodius Centaurs had passed her by, she stood up and cautiously stepped out of the shelter of the cave. She had just started working her way over and under the fallen branches that sheltered the opening of the cave when she heard her name.

"Carling."

Someone was calling her from within the stone crevasse. She stopped, her heart pounding, and slowly turned around. She took in a quick breath even as she stumbled backward, falling over a branch that lay on the ground, concealed by the snow.

The opening to the cave, which had previously been so dark she couldn't see past the first foot or so, was now glowing with a bright, yellow light. She heard her name again.

"Carling."

This time she recognized the voice and her heart leaped for joy. "Wizard? Is that you?"

"It is I," Vidente said as he stepped out of the opening of the cave, bringing his bright light into the dark forest like a lighthouse in a storm. The tall, thin wizard was wearing his customary long cloak. The hood covered his head, concealing his brown hair. But this time, his body was radiating a bright light that even the thick cloak could not conceal. A broad smile filled his narrow face, and his neatly trimmed brown beard seemed to be dancing with pleasure as he spoke.

Carling was so happy to see him that she wanted to run to him and hug him. But she dared not, fearing that wouldn't be appropriate. Instead, she stretched forth her hands and walked toward him, her violet eyes twinkling.

As she approached, the Wizard of Crystonia smiled down at her, causing the wrinkles at the sides of his penetrating blue eyes to deepen.

"I have been waiting for you to return," Carling said quietly.

"I know you have, my dear. But I wanted you to continue with your training."

Carling nodded. "Am I ready for my next quest?"

"Yes. I think you are." As he said this the Wizard smiled and rubbed his beard. Carling scratched her head. She was sure his beard had been long and gray the first time she met him. She also noticed that his cheeks became even more prominent when he smiled. He was very handsome in a fatherly sort of way, a fact not lost on Carling.

Suddenly his face froze and he looked beyond her in the direction that the Centaurs had gone. "Step inside the cave. Quickly!" With a swish of his cape, Vidente disappeared and darkness returned to the interior of the cavern.

Carling did as she was told and not a moment too soon. The instant she was secreted away in the darkness, she heard pounding hoof beats crashing through the forest. The Heilodius Centaurs were returning. Had they reached her village? She hoped not. And was Higson safe? She hoped so.

The Heilodius Centaurs passed quickly. Carling watched them go. Their bows and arrows were still in their hands, but Carling saw no signs of injuries or killed game. She tilted her head to one side and rubbed her chin. What had they done in the short time since they first passed her by?

After the sound of hooves crushing leaves and branches disappeared, the cave became light again. Carling turned. The Wizard of Crystonia was standing in the cave.

"You never left, did you," Carling stated, her heart pounding in her chest.

He smiled. "I do have some talents that come in quite handy."

"What are the Heilodius Centaurs doing here?" Carling said, her voice trembling.

"Just going about causing trouble, I suspect."

Her mind leaped back to her reason for being in the forest in the first place, and to Higson. "Higson. He's in the forest alone."

"As are you, my dear."

"I'm not alone. I have you."

The Wizard smiled and stretched forth his bejeweled hands, cradling her face.

"Do not worry about your friend. I have the feeling he can take care of himself." The tall wizard winked one of his kind, shining eyes and dropped his hands. "Now, my dear Carling, it is time to send you on another quest to gather the next stone for the Silver Breastplate."

Carling's hand went to the breastplate and felt the green Stone of Mercy that it held. Then she moved her hand to each of the three spaces designed to hold additional stones...stones that would give her the power to rule the land of Crystonia righteously.

The Wizard continued. "The stone you will be sent to acquire is the beautiful red Stone of Courage."

Vidente paused and smiled. He stepped up to her and placed his hands with their beautiful rings gently on her shoulders. Looking into her eyes, he said, "As the future leader of Crystonia you will face fear, experience ridicule, and meet opposition, even from those you count as your friends. But you must have the courage to stand for principles of righteousness even if that means defying the consensus. Having the virtue of courage will be necessary as you move forward, striving to live and lead as you should."

"Where shall I seek this stone?"

"It will be found in the Northern Reaches."

Carling gasped. No Duende she had ever known had ventured into the Northern Reaches, the foreboding and uncharted land to the north of the great Mount Heilodius. Of course, most of the Duende she knew had not ventured anywhere.

The Wizard looked down at her. Carling beheld that his eyes were soft and kind. "The stone is being guarded by one of my servants, a Tommy Knocker by the name of Shim."

"A Tommy Knocker? I know of no such species."

Vidente's face became impassive. "I do believe Shim is the only one of his kind. He is quite a recluse, which is why I picked him to guard the Stone of Courage. My only concern is that he has become quite attached to the stone and may not be very excited about giving it up. I fear he may not be as cooperative as the great eagle

Baskus was about turning the Stone of Mercy over to you."

"But I have always been told the Northern Reaches was a vast, impenetrable region. How will I ever find a tiny stone in such a large and rugged place?"

"Find the Cave of the Bats. If you find that cave, you will find Shim. I believe bats are Shim's only friends," Vidente said. In the blink of an eye, the Wizard of Crystonia disappeared.

"Have I told you I hate the way you do that?" Carling said into the darkness.

There was no response.

CHAPTER 3

The Second Quest Begins

CARLING PEEKED OUT OF the cave to make sure the Heilodius Centaurs were gone. Confident she was safe, she dashed through the forest toward the village of Duenton, concern for both Higson and the other Duende momentarily pushing aside thoughts of the new assignment she had just been given.

Once she got to the village, she found Higson waiting by the large city gates on the west side of the walls Carling had designed, walls that had turned the village into a fortress. The massive entry was the only way in and out of the village of Duenton. The artisans in the village had worked hard to make it pretty, even though Carling kept stressing that it had to be utilitarian and strong. Thick planks of wood were bound together with metal bands. But the wood planks had beautiful carvings of trees sculpted into them, and the bands were anything but plain. They twisted and turned across the wooden doors like an unruly vine.

On either side of the doors, stone watch towers stood as silent sentries. It was in these towers that the Fauns were stationed at all times to act as guards. The Fauns, half human and half goat, had helped Carling on her previous quest in return for her assistance with escaping from enslavement to the Cyclops. Now they worked to help protect the village of Duenton.

Higson ran toward Carling as soon as she stepped out of the forest. "Carling! Carling! I've been so worried about..." He stopped in mid-sentence. "What is it? I can see it in your eyes. Something has happened. Tell me."

Carling let out a deep breath, so relieved was she to see both her friend and the village safe. "Am I that transparent?" she said, forcing a smile.

"I know you too well. Now out with it."

For a moment, her thoughts returned to the appearance of Vidente in the cave. "The Wizard came to me."

"Ah. I understand. So, you didn't see the Heilodius Centaurs?"

"Yes. They passed right by me. I was worried about you and the village! Did they reach Duenton?"

"It was the strangest thing. I was just returning from hunting when I heard the commotion. I hid in the woods and watched. All they did was gallop around the walls of the village, shouting. No arrows were shot."

"That *is* strange," Carling said with a slight shake of her head.

"I thought so, too. Perhaps they just wanted to scare us. Perhaps they were scoping out our defenses."

"How did the guards and villagers react?" Carling asked.

"Perfectly. The gates were shut immediately. Everyone was safe inside. Everyone, that is, except you and me. The Fauns didn't even shoot an arrow...they just remained calm and waited to see what was going to happen. You would have been proud of them."

Carling smiled, pleased.

"Now," Higson said, "tell me about the Wizard's visit."

"We have a new quest."

The next afternoon when Tibbals and Tandum arrived for sparring practice, Carling had a written list of things for everyone to do.

"Before I pass this out," she began, "I need to know if the two of you are willing to accompany me to gather the second stone."

Tibbals burst into tears.

Carling rushed over to her and put her arms around her, at least as far up as she could reach. "Tibbals. Tibbals. You don't have to accompany me on another quest. I will understand and still love you."

Tibbals sniffed and wiped her eyes with her hand. Taking a deep breath, she spoke between sobs. "No. You don't understand." Sob. "Of course I will go with you." Sob. "How could you think for a moment that I wouldn't?" Sob. "It's just that...well...last time was so awful! What if it's like that again?"

Carling lowered her gaze. Images of their days in the prison beneath Fort Heilodius filled her mind. She felt her eyes start to sting. Holding back her own tears, she said, "Tibbals, I can't promise that it won't be awful. The Wizard said we have to go to the Northern Reaches."

Tibbals gasped as Tandum started. "The Northern Reaches?" he said, clearly shocked. "I don't know if any Centaur has been there before."

"I mean it when I say I would understand if you don't want to come," Carling repeated.

Tandum stepped up and gave Carling a hug. "We will go. We just need to get used to the idea. Isn't that right, Tibbals?"

Tibbals took a deep breath to compose herself. "When do we leave?"

"That's my baby sister," Tandum said.

A late spring drizzle fell from the low-hanging clouds as Carling and Higson mounted their Centaurs. Strapped to their backs were packs filled with everything they thought they might need. Bows, quivers filled with arrows, and swords in sheaths were strapped on the outsides of the packs. The Fauns at the watchtowers to the village bid them a tearful farewell.

Pik, the Faun who'd helped Carling save her friends in Manyon Canyon and then rescued her from the prison beneath Fort Heilodius, stood at the gate as they passed through. "Are you sure you don't want me to come with you?" he asked, looking up at Carling.

Carling shook her head from her perch atop Tibbals. "Thank you, Pik. But you are needed here to keep the villagers safe. It is very likely that the Heilodius Centaurs are planning another attack. You must be ready. Besides, it would be impossible for you to keep up with Tibbals and Tandum."

"True that," he said. "Godspeed, my dear friend. Return to us soon."

The first stop was in the city of Minsheen, home to the Minsheen herd. The group wanted to consult with the Centaur named Adivino. This wise, old stallion was the herd's historian. He had helped Carling on her quest to find the green Stone of Mercy. Tibbals and Tandum were sure he could give them some much-needed advice that would help them find the Tommy Knocker named Shim.

They entered the old Centaur's cottage when beckoned by Adivino's cheerful voice. They stepped into a small square room with several nooks and crannies tucked here and there. Most of the walls were lined with shelves overflowing with books and scrolls. Adivino was sitting at his desk in front of a roaring fire. He held up his hand to signal the need for silence as he continued writing. His quill pen made scratching sounds as he wiggled it across the parchment roll that was spread out in front of him on the desk. Carling watched and waited, knowing full well not to interrupt Adivino in the middle of his important work of recording the history of the Centaurs.

A few minutes later, the Centaur historian stopped writing, set down his pen, and pressed a blotter over the ink. He held up the scroll and examined it through his spectacles. Apparently satisfied with his work, he sighed, set the scroll back on his desk, and turned to face his guests, finally able to give them his full attention.

Adivino smiled broadly, his pale blue eyes twinkling. "I'm delighted to see all of you! To what do I owe the honor of your visit?"

Carling stepped forward. "Adivino, the Wizard of Crystonia has sent me on a new quest."

Adivino nodded and ran his fingers through his long beard. "I see. I see. You are to gather the next stone. Is that correct?"

Carling smiled weakly. "Yes" she said.

"And which stone has Vidente sent you to find?"

"The Stone of Courage."

"Ah-h-h, yes. A wise choice. A wise choice, indeed." The Centaur unfolded his long legs from the couch that was set in front of his desk, stood up, and stepped over to the fireplace. He took an iron poker and stirred the logs to rejuvenate the failing flames. Slowly, he set the metal tool back on the hearth and turned around. Carling waited to hear what he was going to say next, well aware that Adivino could not be rushed.

"What do you want from me, my dears?" asked the ancient Centaur.

Tandum stepped forward. "We seek any help or advice you can give us."

Adivino nodded, his lips pressed in a thin line as his fingers stroked his beard. Turning to face Carling, he asked, "Has Vidente told you where to seek this stone?"

"The Wizard told me that Shim, a Tommy Knocker residing in the Northern Reaches, has been guarding it."

Adivino sucked in his breath and blinked. His fingers found his long beard again. "Shim, is it? Well that is, indeed, a surprise. An interesting choice for a guardian, I must say. I'm sure the Wizard has his reasons for doing what he does even if we mere mortals don't always understand them."

Adivino took in another deep breath and shook his head, swishing his tail at the same time. "Well, then. Let us get the help we need." The Centaur turned on his haunches and walked quickly to a shelf on the far side of the room. The shelf was piled high with dusty scrolls that appeared to be stuffed in place without rhyme or reason. Yet Adivino bent over and pulled out just the roll he desired without hesitation.

He walked across the cottage, his hooves clicking on the wooden boards that covered the floor, and unrolled the scroll across a large, rough-hewn table. Carling and Higson stood on the tips of their toes and even then could just barely see over the edge. With their chins hooked on the table, they looked at the unrolled scroll.

"This is a map of Crystonia," Adivino said as he smoothed out the aged parchment with his long, wrinkled hands. He pointed to the top of the map. "This entire region is what we call the 'Northern Reaches.' We know very little about the area, actually. Very few of us have spent any time exploring it. It is quite rugged, and cold. However, I once had the opportunity to be of service to the Ice Horses who often graze on the glaciers that cover the north face of Mount Heilodius. They travel all around the region in search of fresh ice to nourish their bodies."

"Ice Horses?" asked Tibbals.

"Yes, my dear," Adivino said. "They are our very distant cousins, and quite beautiful, I might add."

"This land gets stranger and stranger the more I learn about it," exclaimed Carling.

"Yes, little Duende," chuckled the wise old Centaur. "You have been quite sheltered in your little village. There is a big world out there just waiting for you to discover."

"How might the Ice Horses help us?" asked Tandum.

"Since they are quite familiar with the area, I'm sure they could help you find Shim."

"Vidente said Shim was in the Cave of the Bats," added Carling.

Adivino folded his arms across his chest. "The Cave of the Bats...The Cave of the Bats? Hum-m-m. I really don't know much about the Northern Reaches, having never set hoof in the region—never had the desire to, I might add. So I know nothing of such a cave. But if you can find the Ice Horses, I would not be surprised if they could lead you right to it. This time of year they will be lower down on the north side of Mount Heilodius."

Adivino rolled up the map. Carling wished she had more time to examine this land that she was destined to rule and made a mental note to return to Adivino's cottage and study the map at length. For now, she lowered herself back onto the soles of her feet and stepped away from the table.

"Thank you for your help, Adivino," she said. "We will follow your counsel and find the Ice Horses."

"It's getting late," added Tandum. "We had best be on our way."

"May the power of the Centaurs go with you, my dear Carling. And with all of you," said Adivino as they turned to hurry out of the cottage.

Carling was the last to leave. She was just about to step through the doorway when Adivino called out to her. "And Carling...beware the Ogres."

Carling's eyes opened wide as she turned back to look at him.

Adivino nodded. "Beware the Ogres," he repeated.

CHAPTER 4

Journey to the Northern Reaches

WHILE TIBBALS AND TANDUM dashed back to their home in the center of the city of Minsheen to gather warm clothing, Higson and Carling waited in the town square. The two little Duende climbed up on a park bench designed for a Centaur. It was high and wide—just right for Centaurs to fold their legs beneath them and lay down to relax. Carling and Higson, on the other hand, were forced to perch on the front edge of the bench and dangle their legs over the side.

As they waited, Carling looked around at the beautifully designed and well-built stores and stables that made up the city of Minsheen. Their white walls glistened in the sun. Their roofs were covered with gold, which added both a touch of sparkling color and elegance. The doors were painted in bright colors and set into intricately carved doorframes. The structures here were far more splendid than the little buildings in the village of Duenton.

Carling watched Centaurs from the Minsheen herd pass by, their hooves beating out a staccato rhythm on the cobblestone streets. Some rushed past on apparently important errands. Others strolled by in couples, hand in hand, tails swishing, the mares giggling. Many smiled and waved at the two young Duende, whom they viewed as heroes because Carling and Higson had saved several local fillies' lives. Tibbals was one of the fillies Carling and Higson had saved, and their friend had expressed her gratitude to them many times.

Carling watched the Centaurs and smiled. She turned to Higson, whose silence indicated he was lost in his own thoughts. "Well, here we go again, Higson. Another adventure."

Higson frowned. "Let's hope we don't end up in a prison cell this time."

Carling reached over and took Higson's hand. "Thank you for always being here for me," she said, her gaze capturing his.

Higson pursed his lips and looked away.

Carling's heart sank, and she could feel her hand sweating as it clasped his. "What is it? What's bothering you?"

Higson looked down and kicked the back of his heels against the side of the bench.

Carling's heart ached. "Can you ever forgive me for the loss of your parents?"

"I know it wasn't your fault. You did what you had to do. It's just that..."

"...it hurts so much." Carling finished his sentence as tears escaped her violet eyes.

Higson nodded. He set his jaw, lifted his chin, and turned to the north. "But we have an important task to perform. We can't let our pain and sorrow get in the way."

Carling flung her arms around her best friend and hugged him tightly. "I can't do this without you," she whispered.

Suddenly remembering Adivino's last warning, she pushed back and looked Higson in the eye. "What do you know about Ogres?"

"Ogres? Why do you ask?"

"Adivino told me to beware of them."

Higson nodded, his face taking on a solemn expression. "I've heard they are very large, very stupid, and want to rule Crystonia."

"Where do they live?"

Higson sucked in a quick breath of air as a realization struck him. "In the Northern Reaches."

The journey to the Northern Reaches was anything but easy. They needed to work their way through the Forest of Rumors and past Mount Heilodius to arrive in the unknown land said to be the home of Shim the Tommy Knocker.

The spring rains had left the ground saturated. Tibbals's and Tandum's hooves sank deep in the mud with each step. The wet earth gripped their hooves, and they had to struggle to lift each hoof to take another step. The overhanging trees released their collection of raindrops on their heads and backs. Soon, all of them were soaked. But Carling couldn't help but notice how fresh and clean the forest smelled, and she breathed in deeply as they moved between the trees, carving their own path on what was, for them, unchartered territory. The deeper into the Forest of Rumors they traveled, the more dense the trees and brush became. The travelers eventually found themselves walled in on both sides by the wild trees and brush. The air became thick and still.

They trudged on, making slow progress, talking about anything but the fears in their hearts. Tibbals complained about the mud staining her beautiful white stockings that covered the lower sections of her four legs. Tandum and Higson talked about their favorite hunting exploits. Carling sat on Tibbals's back and braided the filly's long, pale, yellow tresses in an attempt to distract herself from her fears. It didn't work very well.

Once they reached higher and firmer ground, Carling felt like they were finally free again, released from the thick mud, dense vegetation, and oppressive air. Tibbals and Tandum were able to pick up a rolling canter. Perched securely on Tibbals's back, Carling lifted her face toward the sun and reveled in the feeling of the wind as it brushed her cheeks and tossed her auburn hair. It felt as if the wind had come straight from heaven. Riding on the back of a cantering Centaur gave her a feeling of freedom that couldn't be matched.

As the group reached the top of a hill, the trees parted and they caught their first glimpse of Mount Heilodius. Carling caught her breath and her hand flew to her mouth as she gazed at the enormous but magnificent mountain.

The Centaurs came to an abrupt halt and Carling glanced at Higson and Tandum. Judging from the expressions on their faces, it was clear that the mountain brought up an extreme mixture of emotions for them. Carling felt the same way and imagined Tibbals did as well. While Carling knew the mountain was the site of her future home as the queen of Crystonia, it also reminded her of the terrible days she and her companions had spent in the dark, dank prison cells beneath the fortress walls of Fort Heilodius. This ramshackle city, situated at the base of Mount Heilodius on its southern slopes, was the home of the Heilodius Centaurs. This band of rebels split off from the Minsheen herd because of their desire to secure the throne and rule of Crystonia for themselves. Carling felt fear grip her more tightly as her heart began pounding heavily in her chest.

Without saying a word, Tibbals and Tandum started down the north side of the hill.

Carling pulled her thoughts away from the Heilodius Centaurs and forced herself to focus on their mission. She had no illusions that finding the red Stone of Courage would be easy. The Wizard had warned her the Tommy Knocker named Shim had become possessive of the stone. This gave her justified cause to worry.

"Duck," shouted Tandum.

The young Duende was pulled from her reverie just in time to avoid getting hit in the head by a low branch.

Higson was not so lucky. The branch struck him right across his forehead and sent him tumbling backward, over Tandum's haunches, and onto the ground. Tibbals and Tandum stopped. Carling leaped from Tibbals's back and ran over to check on her friend.

Higson lay on the ground, holding his head and moaning softly.

"Higson! Higson! Are you alright?" said Carling as she dropped to her knees beside him. Tibbals and Tandum hovered above them.

"Oh-h-h, my head...my head hurts. Am I bleeding?" he asked, his eyes squeezed shut.

Carling gently raised his head. Her hands came away reddened with Higson's blood.

"Um...yes." She quickly added, "But it's not too bad. Just a small cut from hitting a rock."

"I'm sorry, Higson," Tandum said. "It was my fault for not warning you soon enough. And I was probably going too fast as well."

"Why don't we bed down here for the night," Tibbals suggested. "It's getting dark and we can get some shelter under those overhanging rocks," she said, pointing to the side of a cliff on their right.

Carling looked up. Her eyes were opened wide with worry. "We're so close to Fort Heilodius. Do you think we'll be safe here?"

"The Heilodius Centaurs don't even know we're here, so they won't be searching for us," Tandum said. "Regardless, we'll conceal ourselves with branches." He broke off a fir bough.

Tibbals bent down, picked up Higson, and carried him to their makeshift shelter. Once beneath the rocky overhang, Carling and Tibbals cleaned Higson's wound with water and cloth from their packs and bedded their friend down on a soft bed made of moss and leaves.

Tandum, as promised, built a wall of branches, completely concealing the little group.

After a meager meal of cheese and dried meat from her pack, Carling curled up on the leaf-covered floor of their shelter. She pressed her back against the stone wall and was soon asleep, her dreams filled with Ice Horses and Tommy Knockers.

CHAPTER 5

Ice Horses

THE MORNING SUN WORKED its way between the intertwined branches, sending a ray of sunshine across Carling's face. She opened her eyes and looked around without moving. She was wedged between the warm horse-bodies of Tibbals and Tandum. She smelled the sweet aroma of horseflesh combined with Tibbals's perfume. It made her smile.

The moment she sat up, everyone else began moving as well. "We can't sleep the day away," said Tibbals. "Let's get something to eat. I'm starving!"

Carling rolled onto her side to check on Higson. "How's your head feeling?"

"Fine. I'm fine. Don't worry about me," he said, brushing aside her concern with a wave of his hand.

After a breakfast of rolls and fruit from their packs and a long drink in a nearby stream, the two Centaurs were ready to carry their riders for another day. They picked a route that would keep them well to the east of Fort Heilodius. But even so, they kept on the alert for any signs of the dangerous rebels that roamed the forest around Mount Heilodius. They knew the evil Centaurs were quite familiar with the Forest of Rumors that lay between Fort Heilodius and the city of Minsheen, far more familiar than they were.

The further north the group traveled, the more rugged the terrain became. On occasion, they were able to follow deer trails and make good progress. At other times, they were pushing through brush and tree limbs and climbing steep hillsides. Sometimes they would come to a dead end at the edge of a steep cliff and would have to backtrack. They kept their bearings, however, by keeping Mount Heilodius on their left in their attempt to move around it and find the glaciers on its north face, where they hoped to find the Ice Horses.

By the time the travelers were in the shadow of the mountain, the temperature had dropped considerably. Carling looked up and saw the threatening dark clouds. She could smell snow on the wind and the cold air stung her nostrils. They were trotting right into a spring snowstorm.

She wrapped her cloak more tightly around her and tried to cover her pointed ears with its hood. The Duende felt Tibbals shiver beneath her. She reached into her bag, took out a scarf, and gently wrapped it around Tibbals's neck. It wasn't long before tiny flakes of snow were kissing all of their cheeks.

As they climbed higher up the sides of Mount Heilodius, the air got colder and the snowflakes got bigger. The white blanket that covered the forest floor made travel hard, and Tibbals and Tandum found themselves tripping over hidden branches and rocks.

The roar of a waterfall bounced between the trees, prompting Carling to cringe at the thought of having to cross an icy-cold mountain stream. She pulled her cloak tighter around her body and glanced over just in time to see Higson doing the same. Tandum's and Tibbals's clothes were wet from the snow and their own perspiration due to so many hours of exertion. Carling frowned and rubbed Tibbals's shoulder. "Are you alright?" she asked.

"I'm having a hard go of it, that's for sure," Tibbals answered between huffing and puffing to catch her breath. "I'm looking for some place to get out of this snow, but I haven't seen anything yet."

Carling squinted through the falling snow, looking for some sort of shelter. Nothing. She sighed and felt her body shiver.

Just ahead, Carling saw the rushing water of the mountain stream dissecting their path. The Centaurs stopped at the water's edge.

"Great," said Tandum with a snort.

"Which way should we go, big brother?" Tibbals asked, turning her head back and forth to look in both directions.

"Your guess is as good as mine," he replied, frustration evident in his voice.

"Come toward me." A musical voice floated in the air.

Startled, the two Duende and the two Centaurs looked up. At that very moment, a gust of wind lifted the snowflakes long enough to clear their view. Standing on the far side of the stream was a pure white horse. His body sparkled and his white eyes twinkled. His mane and tail looked like icicles, and the feathering around his hooves looked as though it had been sculpted by an artist. He was truly magnificent.

Carling's eyes bulged as her hand flew to cover her gaping mouth. Tibbals let out a squeal of surprise. Tandum and Higson barely moved.

"An Ice Horse," Tibbles exclaimed.

"You are searching for us, no doubt, my young ones. Well, come toward me." The Ice Horse smiled kindly. "Step to the river. I will take care of you. Trust me."

The four travelers looked back and forth at one another.

"Do we trust him?" Tibbals whispered.

"I think we should," answered Carling. "Adivino wanted us to find them."

"Okay, then," said Tandum as he lifted his hoof. He hesitated for a moment with his hoof in the air, then lowered it toward the water. As he prepared to enter the water, his head lifted in shock. His hoof hit firm ice. He looked over at the Ice Horse with wide eyes.

"Come to me. Do not doubt," said the glorious creature.

Tibbals and Carling watched with bated breath as Tandum took a second step, then a third and a fourth. With each step, his hooves were held above the raging river on a sheet of ice, a sheet that kept expanding with each step he took.

Carling and Tibbals stood on the shore, watching with their mouths agape. Halfway across, Higson turned back to look at them from where he sat balanced on Tandum's back. "Aren't you coming?" he said with a smile.

Tibbals took a deep breath and placed one dainty hoof on the ice bridge.

Once both Centaurs and their riders were safely on the other side of the river, they approached the Ice

Horse. He was much taller than either of the Centaurs. His white eyes were kind. His nostrils breathed out puffs of steam. His mouth turned up in a smile. "Welcome to the Northern Reaches," he said.

Carling spoke up first. "Adivino sent us to find you."

"Ah-h-h. Adivino sent you, did he? How is that old and wise Centaur doing?"

"Quite well, thank you," added Tibbals.

"And why, may I ask, did he send you here?"

Tandum cleared his throat. "We are on a quest to collect the second stone for Carling's Silver Breastplate."

Carling jerked her head around and frowned at Tandum. She wasn't sure if they should have told the Ice Horse about the Silver Breastplate without Vidente's permission. While all the races in the land of Crystonia knew that the rightful heir to the throne was the one to whom the Silver Breastplate was given, Carling had already learned not everyone wanted that prophecy to be fulfilled. Carling didn't know how the Ice Horses would react.

Tandum looked back at her, raised his eyebrows, and shrugged his shoulders. Perhaps he realized he had spoken out of turn, but it was too late now.

The Ice Horse turned and looked at Carling. "Are you Carling?"

Carling turned her head to face the ice stallion, lowered her gaze, and nodded.

"So *you* are the possessor of the Silver Breastplate," he stated with unconcealed surprise. Clearly he, like everyone else in the land of Crystonia, had not expected the Silver Breastplate to be in the possession of a young Duende girl.

Carling nodded again.

He lowered his large head and looked directly at her. "And you must find a stone to complete the Silver Breastplate? What stone is that?"

"The Stone of Courage," Carling said.

"I see. And you believe it to be in the Northern Reaches?"

"The Wizard of Crystonia, Vidente, told me he had hidden it here."

"Did he give you any other information?"

"Yes. He said the Tommy Knocker, Shim, has been guarding it."

At this, the Ice Horse reared up on his back ice legs and pawed the air with his front ice hooves. "That nasty creature!" he said as he lowered himself back down. "Why would the Wizard leave it with him?"

"I don't know," said Carling, suddenly feeling defensive. "But he is wiser than we, so we trust he has his reasons."

"Well, I suppose so, but I must say his reasons escape me."

Tandum jumped in. "Adivino told us you might know where we can find Shim?"

"Yes. He has made a home for himself in the Cave of the Bats."

Carling nodded. "That's what Vidente told me."

"It's a nasty place, I must say. I don't envy you going there."

"Do you know where this cave is?" inquired Tibbals.

"Oh, yes. I know the Northern Reaches like the back of my hoof."

"Would you be so kind as to lead us to this cave, then?" asked Tibbals, batting her eyelashes and smiling demurely.

Carling smiled to herself and wondered if Tibbals's skill with flirtation would work on an Ice Horse.

Apparently it did, for he answered right away. "I would be honored to lead you there. But I must tell you, once we get there, I will not go in. It is not a place I dare enter."

Carling and Higson exchanged worried glances.

The Ice Horse turned on his haunches as he said, "Follow me." He started down the glacier that covered the north face of Mount Heilodius and Tibbals and Tandum followed. Soon they passed a large mound of snow. Just as they were beside the large pile, it started to shake violently. Through the flying snow, another Ice Horse appeared, shaking his mane that looked and sounded like icicles tinkling together as they bounced from one side of his thick neck to the other.

"Crystal, who do we have here? And where are you taking them?" the newly arrived Ice Horse said.

Motioning toward Carling, the Ice Horse apparently named "Crystal" tossed his head toward Carling and said, "This is the bearer of the Silver Breastplate. She and her companions have been sent by the Wizard to collect the Stone of Courage. They are seeking it in the Cave of the Bats. I am leading them to the cave."

"Well, it certainly will take some courage to go there," the new Ice Horse responded as he tossed his head and swished his tail. "May I accompany you to the cave?"

"We would love to have you come along," said Carling, even as she felt her anxiety increase at the thought of going to the cave. She felt a little safer surrounded by these strange and beautiful creatures.

Higson nodded and added his agreement. "It would be good to have you join us."

They were soon joined by several other Ice Horses. The pure white creatures were like any herd of horses. Some were playful, some bossy, others reserved, and still others cautious. As they moved lower, the snow stopped and the air welcomed them by becoming slightly warmer, warmth they had been missing while in the frigid air near the mountain peak. However, the warmer temperatures during the day had melted the top of the snow, only to have the frigid nights refreeze it into a layer of ice that was very slick. Tibbals was having trouble keeping her feet underneath her as she slipped along behind Crystal.

Suddenly, Crystal stopped and turned to face them. "Are you ready for some fun?" he asked, smiling so broadly that his white teeth glistened in the sun.

Carling and her friends looked back and forth at one another, none of them sure just what the Ice Horse meant.

"Follow me," Crystal said as he spun around and dropped to his haunches in a sitting position. Pushing off with his front hooves, Crystal let out a hoot and holler and disappeared down the hill.

"Wow!" exclaimed Higson.

One of the other Ice Horses pushed past them and followed Crystal's lead. With excited whinnies, she, too, disappeared down the hill.

"Let's go," said Tandum. "Hold on, Higson."

Tandum dropped to his haunches, pushed off, and began sliding.

Tibbals giggled. "This looks fun," she said to Carling. "Are you ready?"

Carling laughed. "I guess so."

Tibbals sat down on her haunches, her long tail flowing out behind her. She pushed off and began sliding down the glacier. The Ice Horses must have done this before as they were all sliding down a clearly defined track, complete with banked turns.

Laughing with delight, the filly and her Duende friend whizzed down the hill. Carling felt her stomach leap to her throat as they dropped down the glacier, gaining speed with every inch. They zoomed first one way, then the other. As they slid up the side of one banked turn, Carling clutched Tibbles tightly, fearing they would go over the edge. But around the corner they went and continued down the hill.

The cold air kissed their cheeks and turned their noses red while bringing tears to their eyes. Carling could barely see anything through the tears as they sped down the hill. The little Duende couldn't remember having had this much fun for a long time. By the time they reached the bottom of the glacier, they crumpled into a pile of hooves and feet while laughing so hard their jaws and stomachs hurt.

"Can we do that again?" Carling asked once she'd caught her breath.

"Not if you ever want to reach the Cave of the Bats. But I'm glad you had fun," responded Crystal. "Now move out of the way. Here come some more of my herd."

Carling and Tibbles scrambled to one side just as another Ice Horse slid to a stop right in front of them.

"I don't know when I've had more fun," Carling exclaimed between bursts of laughter as she watched the other Ice Horses slide down and join them.

"Nor I," added Higson, still catching his breath from laughing just as hard as Carling.

For several minutes, the band of travelers talked excitedly about the ice slide. And for those same minutes, Carling was able to forget the seriousness of the quest she was on. It was a welcome interruption.

Finally, all thoughts returned to the task at hand. Brushing off and standing up, the Centaurs, Duende, and Ice Horses got ready to complete their journey. They still had a long way to go to reach the cave. Carling took a deep breath, brushed her curls out of her face, and said, "Let's go."

The Northern Reaches was, indeed, a rough and hostile terrain. The group of travelers left the snow and ice behind as they moved lower. But that was replaced by sharp rocks and boulders. After a while, Carling could feel Tibbals limping as she picked her way over the rocky path on which the Ice Horses were leading them. "Do you want me to get off and walk beside you?" Carling asked, concerned for her friend.

"No, I'm fine. My hooves are just a bit sore," Tibbals responded with a flick of her tail.

Carling swung her leg over Tibbals's back and slid to the ground. "I'll walk beside you, my dear friend," she said, patting the Centaur on the shoulder.

It was slow going through the rest of the day. Carling turned her head and watched the sun hesitate on the horizon before plunging down behind the serrated peaks to the west. Undeterred by the darkness and energized by the increasing cold, the Ice Horses continued on. The group of travelers kept moving throughout the night and into the next day. Carling wondered how long they could keep up this pace. She was exhausted and hungry and was sure Higson, Tibbals, and Tandum were, too. But she said nothing and kept going. It was midday of the second day with the Ice Horses before their guides stopped in front of a tall, jagged cliff.

Motioning with his head, Crystal, their guide, said, "The Cave of the Bats is high up on this cliff. There is a narrow path that weaves its way up the side of this rock face. It ends at the mouth of the cave. Be careful. The trail is treacherous." With a smile and a twinkle of his white eyes, he added, "This is where we leave you. It has been an honor to serve our future queen and her friends," he said, bowing to Carling but looking at Tibbals.

Carling wrapped her arms around the freezing body of the Ice Horse. "Thank you, Crystal. We would never have found this without your help."

The Ice Horse chuckled. "Oh, I'm sure you would have found it. But it probably would have taken you several years!"

Carling smiled. "Then let me thank you for saving us so much time!"

With whinnies and snorts, the Ice Horses galloped away in the direction from which they had come, probably heading back to the glacier and the frigid temperatures that sustained them.

CHAPTER 6

Cave of the Bats

THE FOUR TRAVELERS WATCHED the Ice Horses go. While no one said anything, Carling was sure each was feeling some degree of sorrow. They had all enjoyed their company. Any friendly company is always welcome, after all.

Once the Ice Horses were out of sight, Carling passed her hand over her forehead as though to brush away her reverie. She stepped over and put her hand on Higson's shoulder. "Shall we go first?" she said, pushing herself to take a leadership position that was hard for her.

"Might as well!" he said with a shrug.

"So why do you think the Ice Horses won't go into the cave?" asked Tibbals.

"I don't know. I was wondering that myself. Maybe they just don't like bats," said Carling.

"I can understand that. I don't like them much, either," she replied as she tossed her long blond hair over her shoulder.

"Well, let's go find out what's in this cave," said Higson as he took Carling's hand and gently pulled her forward.

Carling felt herself get tense and for a moment resisted Higson's pull. Then she took a deep breath, looked up to the top of the jagged stone wall, and stepped forward.

Already tired from the three days of traveling through the forest and mountains, they made slow progress up the side of the cliff. Each foot and hoof had to be placed carefully so no one stumbled and fell on a loose rock. On occasion, a misstep sent a rock bouncing down the side of the cliff. Each time that happened, the climbers stopped and watched it descend, grateful it was only a rock and not one of them that was falling.

As they moved higher and higher up the cliff, Carling noticed several clumps of purple flowers clinging to the rock. "Tibbals, what kind of flowers are those? Do you know? I've seen it on the slopes of the hogback to the west of Duenton."

Tibbals took her eyes off the path long enough to look at the flowers. "I think that is Nightspell."

"Nightspell? Isn't that the flower that was fed to the Fauns by a stranger? The poison from that flower nearly killed them."

"You're right. Interesting that we should find it here in the Northern Reaches."

"Yes, it is odd," said Carling. She hadn't thought about who had poisoned the Fauns for a long time. They had told her only that a stranger had given them water. Now Carling began to wonder anew who that stranger might have been and why he would have tried to kill the Fauns.

Perhaps Nightspell was more common throughout the kingdom of Crystonia than she had previously thought.

From the base of the jagged rock crag, they had not been able to see the mouth of the cave, concealed as it was by the scraggly pines that clung tenaciously to the side of the cliff. Trusting in the directions given by the Ice Horses, they kept climbing.

Eventually, a gaping black hole in the side of the stone wall became visible between the tree boughs. They kept their eyes looking downward on the pathway most of the time, but periodically each of them looked up toward what appeared to be the entrance to a cave to check their progress. To Carling, it seemed as though they were making no headway at all. She sighed, dropped her chin, and continued up the path, placing one sore and tired foot ahead of the other and repeating –over and over again.

Once they finally reached the mouth of the cave, it was immediately apparent to Carling why the Ice Horses stayed away from it. A hot wind blew out of the opening of the cave from somewhere deep inside. The poor Ice Horses would have melted in minutes.

Carling stopped in front of the opening to the cave and waited until all her friends were gathered together and had a chance to catch their breath. "Well, here we are. Is everyone ready and willing to go in?" she asked.

"That's what we came for," said Tandum matter-of-factly.

Tibbals twisted her long hair into a knot at the base of her neck. "I really hope the bats don't get caught in my hair. That would be such a mess!"

Tandum rubbed Higson's short, wavy hair. "You worried about that, too, Higson, my friend?"

Higson brushed Tandum's hand away. "Yeah, right!"

"You boys just don't know how hard it is being beautiful all the time. Do they, Carling?"

Carling chuckled. It seemed that Tibbals could always make her smile even when she was filled with so much apprehension. She loved the musical sound of Tibbals's giggles. She wished she could return to being the lighthearted young girl she had been before her parents died and the tremendous burden of becoming a queen was placed upon her. Steeling herself, she said with as much boldness as she could muster, "Let's go find Shim." The young Duende pushed her fears deep inside, turned, and led the way into the cave.

Once inside, the heat became more intense, growing with each step. Glowing, lava-like rocks sat in piles every few feet, the source of the warmth. They also provided a welcome orange light that enabled the travelers to see where they were going.

Tandum called out to his companions. "It's hot in here. If the Ice Horses came in, they would be reduced to a puddle of water in no time."

The others nodded in agreement and kept moving forward.

Between the piles of glowing rocks, the base and walls of the cave were quite smooth. Moisture dripped down the sides, making the walls as shiny as mirrors. The water puddled at the base and trickled across the floor, making the surface as slippery as ice.

The air smelled of sulfur, causing Carling's nose to sting and Tibbals to sneeze. It was after one of these sneezing fits that they heard the noise. It started out like a soft hum-m-m-m. As they moved forward, it began to sound like a quiet rumble.

Carling stopped and listened, perspiration from the heat and her fears beading on her forehead. "I hear a strange sound. Why don't all of you wait here while I go ahead to see what it is?"

"You aren't going anywhere without me," said Higson.

"Nor without me," said Tandum.

"Nor me," added Tibbals.

Together they continued on, moving toward the odd sound that seemed to be getting louder and more ominous with each step.

Tandum and Tibbals, with their superior sense of hearing, stopped. Tibbals put a finger to her lips. "I've never heard anything like it," she said.

The strange noise continued to get louder and louder until it sounded almost like thunder rolling toward them. Carling felt her body become tense and her heart start to pound in her chest. She clenched her fists and stared straight ahead through the orange light. Still, she could see nothing that might make such a sound, a sound that was now frightening.

A few more steps forward brought them to a sharp left turn in the pathway. No sooner had they rounded the corner than they came face to face with the source of the rumbling sound. Flying toward them was a huge colony of giant bats. Each bat had a wing span that was as long as two Centaur tails. It was the flapping of these enormous wings that created the now-deafening rumble. The bats' large ears pointed up from the tops of their fur-covered heads. Their enormous mouths were open wide, revealing sharp fangs. Their red eyes stood out on their heads and were staring straight at the group of friends.

Carling realized Tibbals didn't need to worry about these bats getting tangled in her lovely hair. They were not those sort of bats! What they all needed to worry about was getting eaten alive.

As Tibbals screamed and Higson pulled Carling behind him, Tandum grabbed his bow and nocked an arrow.

The Centaur colt aimed and released an arrow, striking the first bat in the chest. The monster fell to the ground with a high-pitched scream. But this did nothing to stop the other bats. Carling and Higson drew their swords. Tibbals pulled an arrow from her quiver. A vicious battle began. Carling stepped in front of Tibbals and swung her sword, lopping off the wing of an approaching bat. The beast crumbled to the floor of the cave, alive but no longer able to join the battle. With his glowing red eyes, he glared at her with fury. His lips curled back, revealing two long and sharp center teeth and two long fangs. He snapped his teeth at her viciously. Carling raised her sword, confident in the training she had received, and jabbed the polished steel into the bat's chest, ending his suffering and his fury.

Tibbals released an arrow just as Tandum did, each dropping still another beast. As though in a choreographed dance, they both reached for another arrow.

Higson had his own challenges as two bats dove for him at once. He spun around, swinging his sword first at one bat, then at the other. The bats dodged his efforts and circled around, diving at him from another direction.

Carling stepped over to help him, attacking the bats from behind when their attention was on Higson. She struck one bat on its back, serving only to anger him. When the creature whirled around and dove for her, she swung her sword over her head and knocked him to the ground. He got back up and flapped his wings enough to reach her chest. His mouth open, he attempted to sink his two sharp fangs into her. With a magical power of its own, the Silver Breastplate sent out a zap and a spark, shocking the advancing bat as it had a Heilodius Centaur when Carling had been a prisoner at Fort Heilodius. The bat shot backward and landed on the floor of the cave in a stunned stupor. Carling wrapped her arms around the Silver Breastplate, grateful that it had the power to offer her such protection.

None of this slowed down the colony of bats, however. It wasn't long before Carling realized that, as she killed or incapacitated one bat, there were three more to take its place. Bats were flying over their heads and diving between the Centaurs' legs. It was difficult for the Centaurs and Duende to tell where to shoot their arrows or swing their swords. Weakened from their long journey and minimal meals, all of them were powered only by the adrenaline born of their strong instinct to survive.

Tandum abandoned his arrows for his sword, not having time to nock an arrow before a new bat came upon him. Seeing this and though she was much more adept at the bow and arrow, Tibbals did the same.

Carling spun around in a circle, clasping her sword tightly, trying desperately to fight back the bats coming at her from all directions. She broke away from the melee and ran farther down the cave to avoid striking one of her own. Just as she anticipated, several of the bats followed her. Gasping for breath, she turned to face her pursuers, glancing only momentarily at Higson and the Centaurs. They each seemed to be holding their own but, clearly, all of them were in a terrible struggle to keep the bats at bay.

She backed up, pressing her back against the damp side of the cave, and readied herself to fight again as the bats approached. She held up her sword and focused her concentration on the nearest bat. Suddenly, she slipped on the wet stones. Her feet flew up and she landed hard on her back. Instantly, several bats were on top of her. Having learned to avoid her torso after seeing the fate of their comrade, their clawed feet clutched her arms and legs.

"Higson! Help me!" she screamed as the bats lifted her into the air.

But Higson could be of no help. He, too, had been captured by the giant bats and was, even now, being carried upside down through the cave a short distance behind Carling.

CHAPTER 7

The Tommy Knocker
Named Shim

THE BATS' CLAWED FEET cut into Carling's arms and legs as they carried her through the increasingly hot and stale air, flying deeper and deeper into the cave. Facing up toward the ceiling, Carling tried her best to struggle free and, at the very least, turn her head to see where they were going. All her resistance did was cause her more pain. She shouted continuously in hopes her friends could hear her and follow. If any of them did hear her and tried to respond, she could not hear them over the sound of the flapping wings of the bats. She only hoped they were safe and able to come after her. She didn't know Higson was right behind her.

After struggling for several minutes, Carling realized she was struggling in vain and gave up. She let her body go limp, clenching her teeth as she endured the pain from the clutching feet digging into her arms and legs. The young Duende dropped her head back, letting her auburn hair hang toward the floor of the cave. She struggled to keep her eyes open in an attempt to see where she was being taken. She realized she had already missed several twists and turns. The bats' up-and-down flying motion made it hard to focus, but she did her best. Turn right. Turn right. Turn left. Take the center tunnel. Turn right. Turn left. Turn left. Eventually, the twists and turns became too much for her to track and Carling gave up.

Deeper and deeper into the hot and foul-smelling cave the bats carried their captive. How far they traveled, Carling could not even guess. Besides the swishing of the bats' wings, all she could hear was the sound of water echoing through the cave as it slithered down the stone walls or dripped from the ceiling. Slick puddles of water pooled on the stone floor.

At last, the bats carried her into a large cavern that was brightly lit, revealing a high ceiling. Glowing white stalactites connecting with stalagmites seemed to act as pillars to keep the ceiling suspended and cast a bluish-white light throughout the grotto. The floor of the cavern was no longer slick, shiny stone. It was covered with a soft, padded, moss-like substance. This served to mute the sound of the bats' flapping wings and the constant dripping of water. Oddly, the air in the great room smelled fresh and clean. The heat had subsided to a much more comfortable temperature here than in the narrow tunnels through which they had traveled.

Carling was carried to the center of the cavern and dropped. She landed with a "humph" on her back. Just as she caught her breath, Higson landed right beside her.

"Higson! Oh, Higson," she squealed in both relief at not being alone and excitement at seeing him alive. She looked over at him with tears rolling down her cheeks.

"You're here. You're alive." Then she paused and looked around. "But where are we and where are Tandum and Tibbals?"

"The last I saw them, they were still fighting off the bats. I don't know where they are now, and I certainly don't know where *we* are."

"Let me enlighten you."

Startled, Carling and Higson jumped and turned around. A short, bent-over creature with a large nose protruding from a wrinkled, whiskered face limped toward them, leaning on a crooked cane. His clothes were colorful, in sharp contrast to the gray walls that surrounded them. His feet were exceptionally large and covered in boots with turned-up toes. He was staring at them with large round eyes the color of the sky. Bushy eyebrows moved upward and downward as he hobbled toward them.

The two Duende said nothing as the creature shuffled through the moss, getting closer to them with each short step. Carling was both terrified and fascinated by the strange creature.

"I am the proprietor of this cave," he said. He smiled, but his smile disappeared almost as quickly as it came. "Who are you and what are you doing here?"

Carling swallowed. Mustering what little courage she could find, she responded. "We are looking for the Tommy Knocker by the name of Shim."

The creature sucked in a quick breath and narrowed his eyes, examining her closely. "I ask again. Who are you?"

"I am Carling, from the village of Duenton. This is my friend, Higson, from the same village. We have been sent here by the Wizard of Crystonia to collect the Stone of Courage."

At this, the creature lifted himself up to his full height, making him only slightly taller than Carling, and roared a great roar from deep within his chest. The stalactites and stalagmites shook. Pebbles fell from the ceiling and sank into the moss. The few bats still in the cavern left their perches and circled over Carling's and Higson's heads. The creature raised his hands toward the bats and said, "It is okay, my pets. I will handle this." Then he dropped his gaze back to the young intruders and, with teeth clenched, said in a voice that sounded more like a growl, "I want you to leave. Leave this instant!"

Carling and Higson scrambled to their feet. "We cannot leave until we have the S-S-Stone of Courage," Carling said, wishing more than ever for some of the courage she hoped the stone would provide.

Instantly, the creature spun around. When he was facing them once again, he was bent over as he had been when they first saw him. His long fingers clutched the cane with both hands and his smile reappeared. "Forgive me. Forgive me, my dears, for being so rude. It is I that you are seeking. I am Shim."

"You? You're Shim?" asked Higson.

The creature bowed. "At your service."

"Then you know Vidente," Carling stated.

"Yes. Quite well."

"And he has entrusted you with the care of the Stone of Courage?" Carling asked.

Shim's smile disappeared again. But this time, he extended his hand toward Carling. "It is my pleasure to meet you. I knew that one day you, or someone else, would come seeking my stone."

Carling took his hand. She started, for it was as cold as the hand of a corpse. "Then you will give it to us?" she asked as a shiver ran through her body.

"Perhaps I will. Perhaps I won't. I shall have to decide later."

"How much later?" Carling said, releasing his hand.

His eyes narrowed again and his eyebrows twitched up and down. "When I have sufficiently tested you to see if you are worthy." He clucked his tongue and muttered, "Such a pity. Such a pity," he said, seemingly to only himself.

Carling's heart gave a terrible jolt. *A test? What could he mean by that?* she wondered.

Higson stepped forward. "That is not your responsibility. Carling has been sent here by Vidente. He, alone, is in charge of the stone. And he decides who should possess it."

A low growl arose from Shim's chest. "We shall see." He spun around again, spinning his cane over his head, and disappeared in a flash of light.

CHAPTER 8

Exploring the Cave

THE SUDDEN APPEARANCE AND disappearance of the odd creature named Shim had been upsetting, and Carling wished she could just go home and forget all about this. Her body began quivering in distress and anger. Higson took Carling in his arms and held her tightly until she quit shaking. She looked at him, her violet eyes wide with both fear and wonder. "What did Shim mean by a test? And what kind of magic are we dealing with?"

"I don't know," her friend said, "but I'm afraid we will soon find out."

Carling shuddered. "I don't understand why Vidente would entrust the stone to such a vile creature."

Higson shrugged as he released his embrace. "He must have his reasons, though those reasons escape me."

"Let's get out of here and find Tibbals and Tandum," said Carling with new determination in her voice.

Together they began exploring the cave. There were numerous tunnels exiting from the large cavern in every direction, and they had no idea from which they had entered. They all appeared alike—the orange glow, the smell of sulfur, the heat. Several giant bats hung from the high ceiling in the middle of the cavern, but no bats were going in and out to give them a hint as to an exit route.

As they moved around the grotto, Carling and Higson came upon a pile of loose rocks that appeared to be covering yet another tunnel. The stack of stones was set back in an arched opening but were stacked so high the two friends could not see beyond the pile.

"What do you suppose is behind those rocks?" asked Higson.

Carling looked at him and raised her eyebrows. "I don't know, but something tells me we should find out."

Higson returned the gaze, his expression skeptical. "What are you going to get us into now? If this is a tunnel, maybe there's a good reason it's blocked off. I'm not sure we should disturb it. Who knows what could be behind there? Besides that, it clearly isn't the way out of here."

Carling bit her lip. Something inside her told her to clear away the rocks. Was it just her natural curiosity or something more? "I don't know why," she said, "but I feel strongly that we should see what's behind these rocks."

Higson let out a loud breath. "Okay, then," he said, shrugging his shoulders in resignation, "let's get to it." He pulled a rock out from the middle of the pile, sending the upper rocks cascading down toward them. They both jumped back to keep from getting hit by the falling stones of various sizes.

Once the rocks settled, they set to work moving the jagged stones away from the entrance. As she worked,

Carling's muscles complained with fatigue and her stomach growled with hunger. But she did her best to ignore these discomforts. She occupied her mind with thoughts of Tibbals and Tandum. *What happened to them? Are they safe? Will they ever be able to find us in this cavern?* Fears and worries threatened to consume her. In response, she worked all the harder.

As the opening became larger, a glowing orange light appeared just as in the other tunnels. Warm air caressed their faces and the smell of sulfur assaulted their noses. It seemed this tunnel was just like all the rest. Why this one would have been blocked off, Carling had no idea. Perhaps it would only take them deeper into the cave. She paused for a moment and pressed her knuckles against her forehead, asking herself why she had been so sure they needed to uncover this opening.

When they cleared most of the rocks away, they looked at each other. Higson nodded. "Do you want me to go first?"

Carling managed a weak smile. "Yes, I do. I'm frightened."

Higson nodded. "I can understand that. I am, too." He paused. "Okay," he said, swallowing hard. "Here goes."

Higson stepped onto the remaining pile of rocks and jumped down to the tunnel entrance. Carling followed. They walked only a short distance before coming to an abrupt stop. Just ahead, stone steps descended into darkness.

"This is definitely not the way out," said Higson. "We didn't come up any stairs to get to Shim's cavern."

"True," Carling said, tucking a limp strand of auburn hair behind one of her dainty pointed ears. "But I have a feeling this is the way to the Stone of Courage."

"But it's completely dark," Higson said, his hands planted firmly on his hips. "We can't see a thing beyond these stairs."

Carling lifted a finger. "I have an idea." She turned around and hurried over to a pile of orange glowing stones. Cautiously, she touched one with the tip of her finger. It felt warm to the touch but not too hot to hold.

She picked up one, turned it over in her hands, examining it carefully, and handed it to Higson. "Our lights," she said with a smile. Then she picked up one for herself.

Higson turned around and started down the stairs, which were now dimly lit by the glowing rock he was holding. Carling followed.

They were just a few steps down when Carling heard a tapping sound. "What's that?"

"What?"

"That tapping sound. Do you hear it?"

Higson stopped and listened. As soon as he did, the tapping stopped. "I don't hear anything."

"It's gone now," said Carling. "I guess it was nothing." But she remained tense, all senses on high alert.

As soon as Higson took another step, the tapping started again.

"There it is! Do you hear it?" said Carling, clutching Higson's shoulder.

"Yes. I do hear it now...it's probably nothing," Higson said, though his wrinkled brow showed that he was worried. "Maybe it's just dripping water."

Carling nodded, swallowing her doubt like a lump in her throat.

The two Duende continued down the stone staircase, walking in rhythm with the tapping. At the base of the long staircase, they found themselves in a narrow tunnel that led straight ahead. The darkness seemed to swallow up what little light the glowing rocks emitted, and they walked forward without any knowledge of what lay ahead. As they walked, the tapping grew louder.

Higson was still in the lead but he stopped suddenly. Carling, who had been watching her feet, bumped into him, nearly knocking him over. He caught himself by grabbing a rock protruding from the wall of the tunnel.

"Look," he said, pointing straight ahead.

It was only now that Carling looked up. They were standing at the edge of a cliff. Ahead of them was a dark abyss, the depth of which they had no way to determine with just the small amount of light they carried with them. Higson bent down and picked up a small rock. He held it over the edge and let it fall. It was a long time before they heard it hit the bottom. The two friends looked at each other, their eyes wide.

"That is a very deep chasm," Carling said. "How will we ever get across it?"

"Are you sure we need to?"

Carling bit her lip and stared straight ahead. *Am I sure?* she asked herself. *I don't know why we are in this tunnel or where it is taking us.* Suddenly a warm feeling came over her like a blanket of spring sunshine and she knew they were in the right place.

"Yes. We need to get across this chasm," she said softly, fear returning and replacing the momentary confidence she had felt.

"Well then...okay," Higson said. He raised his glowing stone to get a better view of the crevasse. It was so deep that the bottom was not visible. But ahead, barely perceptible in the darkness, were several tall stone, tower-like structures. "Look ahead. There are some tall columns that look like stepping stones. I'll bet they are used to get across."

Carling felt her heart skip a beat. "Do you think we can do that? They look awfully far apart. If we miss..." She let the rest of her statement float away into the darkness as her body involuntarily shivered.

Higson reached up to wrap one arm around her. "Don't worry. We can do it. Just think of all the streams in the forest we've crossed by jumping from rock to rock."

She looked down at him and raised her eyebrows with skepticism.

Higson shrugged. "I know it's not *exactly* the same, but I'm sure we can do it."

Carling sucked in a deep breath and let it out with a huff. "Okay, then. Let's do this."

Always the gallant gentleman, Higson offered to go first. Carling wasn't sure she wanted him to, not wanting to see him fall. But as usual he waved aside her protests and stepped back. Taking a deep breath and holding it in his little lungs, Higson took several long strides toward the edge of the abyss and leaped toward the first stone column. Even though his legs were short, he easily made it to the first platform. He turned and smiled at Carling. "See! I told you we can do this, Carling. It looks like the rest of the columns are closer. No big deal!" He turned and leaped toward the next stone, disappearing into the darkness. All Carling could see was a faint orange light from the stone that he carried as it bounced from spot to spot. It wasn't long before even that was swallowed up by the darkness.

Encouraged by Higson's success and motivated by fear of being left alone, Carling jumped toward the first column. She was quite a bit taller than Higson and her legs were much longer. She easily cleared the span from the edge of the cliff to the first stone tower. She could now see the next tower but not Higson. She took a deep breath and jumped toward the second one.

Each of the stone columns was as far apart as Carling was tall. The top of each tower was only about two feet across but was quite flat. Before each leap, Carling narrowed her eyes and aimed her foot to the middle of the next tower. With each successful landing, she paused to take a deep breath and push her auburn curls out of her eyes.

Carling progressed across the deep and dark crevasse one column at a time. Afraid to look down, she kept her eyes on the next stone. She had no idea how much farther ahead Higson was. She couldn't see him. *He must just be several steps ahead,* she thought. She wouldn't let herself think about any other possibility. She continued jumping from rock tower to rock tower. Most of them were in a straight line, but a few were set to one side or another. She had not counted them and had no idea how many she had traversed. Clearly, this was a wide chasm. This far in and with Higson still ahead of her, she had no choice but to keep going.

She felt herself getting weaker, which made each leap harder even though the stone columns seemed to be getting closer together. She landed on one stone that was not level. Instead, it slanted slightly to one side, just enough to cause her to slip and fall to her hands and knees. She hung her head, her hair falling around her face, and gasped for air. The sulfur in the air stung her lungs, and she felt the stinging in her eyes calling forth tears. She took several long breaths through her mouth.

"Carling? Carling? Are you coming?"

Relieved to hear Higson's voice, she lifted her head. Ahead of her just a short distance, Higson's rock glowed softly. Her heart swelled with joy, filling her with a burst of energy. "Higson! I'm here. I'm okay. Are you?" *That was a dumb question*, she said to herself. *If he wasn't okay, he'd be at the bottom of this crevasse!*

"Fine. It's easy the rest of the way," Higson responded.

Carling struggled to her feet, buoyed by Higson's encouragement. She stepped to the edge of the stone pillar and was relieved to see the next stone was just a long step away. The one beyond that was even closer. Soon, she could just walk from stone to stone.

As soon as she reached the far side of deep chasm, she collapsed to the ground and started weeping.

Higson dropped to his knees beside her. "Are you alright?" he said, putting his arms around her.

"No. I'm not alright! We're deep in a dark, hot, smelly cave. I don't know why we're here. And the worst part is I've put you in danger. On top of all that, I don't know where Tibbals and Tandem are or even if they're alive!" She pressed her hands against her eyes as her shoulders slumped. "I don't even want to be a queen. I just want to go home."

Higson sat down beside her and said nothing.

At that moment, the tapping sound they had heard earlier started again. This time, it was very loud. Carling jerked her head up. "That is *not* dripping water."

Ahead, the tunnel continued onward. The sound was clearly coming from that direction. She took a deep breath, wiped the tears from her cheeks, and stood up.

"Is it acceptable if queens cry once in a while?" she asked, sniffing loudly.

"I'm quite sure it is," Higson said. He smiled up at her, then scrambled to his feet.

CHAPTER 9

The Test

FOLLOWING THE SOUND OF the rhythmic tapping, Carling and Higson continued on through the tunnel. Based upon the tunnel's arched configuration and the many small chisel marks on the walls, Carling guessed it had been made by hand, perhaps by the Tommy Knocker named Shim. As they turned a corner, a bright light shone from a short way ahead. Since their eyes had become accustomed to the darkness of the cave, they had to squint to let their eyes adjust to the sudden appearance of so much light. Once Carling could see better, she could tell the tunnel was leading to another large cavern. It was from this part of the cave that the light and sound were coming.

They hurried toward the light and sound but stopped just at the entrance to the grotto. Cautiously they peeked into the cavern. What Carling saw caused her to pull back in fear. It wasn't the source of the tapping that frightened her. It was something else that was the cause of her terror.

Unable to believe her eyes, Carling, with Higson right beside her, slowly peered around the rocky opening of the tunnel. Both jerked back a second time.

Wide-eyed, Carling looked at Higson. "Did you see what I saw?"

Higson, his eyes wide and mouth agape, was clearly too shocked to speak. He merely nodded.

Hanging from a tangled netting made of vines were Tibbals and Tandum. Their forelegs and hind legs dangled through the gaps in the vines, but they were too high up to touch the floor of the cavern. With hands tightly clutching the net, they pressed their faces against the woven vines, the sides of their bodies pressed tightly together. Both Centaurs were staring at the source of the tapping. Neither spoke.

Just below and in front of them stood three stalagmites.

To one side of the cavern, Shim was using the cane Carling and Higson had seen him with earlier to carve into the wall. As he tapped the stone with the tip of the crooked cane, the stick glowed with a bright light and a small amount of the rock wall melted and dripped to the floor, causing the moss that covered the floor like a carpet to sizzle and burn.

Carling heard the thuds of her own heart in her chest keeping pace with Shim's tapping as fear sent a wave of nausea through her body. The young Duende grasped Higson's arm to steady herself.

"What do we do now?" her friend whispered.

Her teeth clenched, Carling let anger overshadow her fear. "We go and have a talk with Shim and find out what this is all about."

Her chin held high, Carling stepped into the grotto. Tibbals saw her, shook her head, and motioned for her to leave. Carling ignored it.

"Shim," said Carling.

Shim stopped tapping and whirled around. "So, you have arrived. I might ask what kept you but that would be rude, now, wouldn't it?"

Carling motioned toward the Centaurs. "Shim, what is the meaning of this?"

Shim smirked as his bushy eyebrows raised so high they nearly disappeared under his cap. With one hand, he rubbed the bristles on his chin as he looked down his large nose. "Well, my dear impetuous girl, since you asked, I will tell you. This is your test."

"My test? What do you mean by that?"

Shim set his jaw and stepped forward, clasping his crooked cane and shaking it in the air.

After watching the cane melt the walls of the cavern, Carling now knew it held magic of its own and eyed it suspiciously.

"So you think you want to be a queen, do you? You think you deserve to possess my beloved Stone of Courage after all I have done to keep it safe?" Not waiting for an answer Shim roared, "Well, prove yourself!" He raised his cane over his head, whirled around, and disappeared. He immediately reappeared on the far side of the cavern, close to where Tibbals and Tandum hung suspended in the netting.

Only now did Carling take the time to examine the situation carefully, and what she saw made her body become rigid and her face turn ashen. Tibbals and Tandum were suspended over a pool of bubbling lava, the source of the sulfur smell and heat that filled the cave. The enormity of the danger her Centaur friends were in caused fear to grip her heart like a vice and squeeze it so tightly she doubted it would ever beat again. Somehow she managed to force enough air out of her lungs to whisper, "Shim, why are you doing this?"

A hideous laugh, the laugh of a madman or a demon, trailed off into a groan. "You have come to take my beloved jewel." He covered his face with his hands, turned away and mumbled to himself, "Such a pity, such a pity."

Higson, who had quietly stood behind Carling during Shim's performance, now lifted his chin, pushed back his shoulders, and stepped toward the creature. "It is not your stone. You are only the caretaker!"

Shim turned back toward them and growled. His face lowered into his scarf, which muffled his response. Looking at Carling with his angry, beady eyes, Shim said, "I will not release my beloved jewel until you have proven yourself to have the courage it takes to be worthy to possess it."

Trying to steady her voice, Carling said, "What do I need to do?"

Shim sprang into life and began dancing around the three sparkling crystal stalagmites that Carling had noticed earlier. But now that she examined them more closely, she noticed each column supported a rough-hewn wooden box. "I have made a fun game for you to play!" Shim said as he let out a giggle that made Carling's blood freeze in her veins. "It is going to be so much fun. Now, let me explain the rules. One of these boxes holds my jewel, my beloved jewel. The other two are empty. If you pick the right box, the stone will be yours. But...," here Shim paused and grinned, hopping from one foot to the other in delight and anticipation, "if you pick one of the empty boxes, your Centaur friends will be dropped into the pool of lava, never to be seen again!"

The creature twirled around the three stone stalagmites, a throaty laughter escaping his lips, his eyes twinkling, his large nose looking even larger.

Carling, frozen in place, followed Shim's dance with her eyes but her mind was busy. *What am I to do? What am I to do, oh Wizard? Tell me, please. This is too much for me.*

Carling could hear Tibbals start to weep. Tandum shouted from the net. "Let Tibbals go! Just take me. She has done nothing to deserve this."

Shim stopped dancing and looked up at his captives. "Oh, she has done quite enough. First, she brought *her* here," he said, pointing his crooked cane at Carling. "And then she killed many of my dear bats. The bats are the innocent ones, after all."

Without saying a word, Carling stepped up to the three columns. The only sound in the cavern was the gurgling of the bubbling lava pool. All eyes were on the young Duende. Carling stopped and held out her hand, stretching it first toward one box then another. Her hand was trembling. With every ounce of patience within her, she waited for some sign from the Wizard to tell her which box to pick.

"What are you waiting for?" screeched Shim. "Pick one! Pick one!"

Carling ignored him and kept waiting for an answer. *Which box? Which box?* She asked over and over. Softly an answer came. It wasn't her ears that were attuned to the response to her pleading–it was something deep inside her that was being touched by some unseen power. Through no effort of her own, her hand moved to the box on her right. Swiftly, she reached out, lifted the latch, and opened the lid, oblivious to the screech coming from Shim.

Nestled in a bed of soft moss was a large red stone.

CHAPTER 10

Escaping Shim's Cave

WITH FLARING NORSTILS AND quivering muscles, Shim bound forward. His hands reached for the stone but, before he was able to grasp his treasure, it disappeared from the box. He stopped, open-mouthed, and stared at the empty case. "My jewel! My beloved jewel! Where have you gone?" he cried, pain laced through his voice and twisting his face.

Slowly, Carling, her heart pounding and perspiration beading on her forehead, pulled back her tunic to reveal the Silver Breastplate. There, nestled securely in what had, just moments before, been an empty hole in the breastplate, sat the red Stone of Courage. It sparkled of its own light. Wide-eyed, Carling looked down at the Silver Breastplate that now held two of the magical Stones of Light. Feelings of wonder and amazement filled her as she looked over at Higson and smiled.

"No-o-o-o-o," cried out Shim upon seeing the stone in the Silver Breastplate. He spun his cane over his head and disappeared.

At the same moment, the room became even brighter. Carling turned around. Standing behind her was the Wizard of Crystonia, Vidente.

"Shim," Vidente said in a quiet but firm voice. "Shim, present yourself."

Shim reappeared, a scowl on his face, his arms folded across his chest.

"Shim, I am not pleased with your behavior," said Vidente.

"You gave *me* the Stone of Courage," Shim snapped.

"It was your duty to protect it until its rightful owner arrived."

"But I *am* its rightful owner. I have sacrificed centuries of my life to guard it. What gives her," he stabbed a finger toward Carling, "the right to come waltzing in here and take it from me? *I* deserve the stone, not her!"

"Enough of this, Shim. You knew it was not your stone to keep," said Vidente, his voice low. Slowly his body rose to an even greater height until his head nearly touched the top of the cavern.

Shim watched the Wizard and a deep groan that sounded more like a growl arose from the Tommy Knocker's throat. He gnashed his teeth like an angry lion.

Carling and Higson stood frozen in place, watching the confrontation play out. Tibbals and Tandum hung from their net, clutching the vines and watching just as intently.

Vidente, his composure intact, fixed the Tommy Knocker with a piercing stare. "Shim, you are to release the Centaurs. Release the Centaurs *now*. Then you may escort your guests out of the Cave of the Bats. No harm may come to any of them, or you will answer to me."

Shim stomped his feet and shook his fists in the air. "I won't! I won't! You can't make me!"

A look of sadness passed over Vidente's face, his eyelids half shielding his bright blue eyes. His beard, which had been white when he first appeared, turned a deep shade of black. Slowly, he stretched forth his hands in fists, pointing the large rings on his middle fingers toward Shim. Two streams of light, one red, one blue, shot from the rings and surrounded Shim. The Tommy Knocker was immediately frozen in place, his fists above his head, his face contorted with anger.

Vidente lowered his hands and slowly shook his head. "You see, Carling, the stones you are gathering have abundant power. But remember, power can be used for great good, or it can corrupt. What you see before you is the latter."

Vidente turned his attention to the Centaurs dangling above the pool of bubbling lava. He smiled sympathetically. "Well, my dear Tibbals and Tandum," he said, "I am sure you would like to be released from your swinging prison."

"Yes, we would really appreciate that," said Tibbals with a nervous giggle.

Vidente directed the power in his rings toward the Centaurs and lowered the net away from the pit of lava and onto the floor of the grotto. The beams of light that flowed forth from the stones melted away the vines.

Tibbals rushed up to Vidente and threw her arms around the Wizard. "Thank you for saving us, Vidente."

The Wizard hesitated, then gently wrapped his arms around her and patted her back. His face was flushed and caressed with a smile. His beard was now a warm yellow color. Carling watched his reaction and wished she was able to be as demonstrative with her emotions as Tibbals.

"Now, my young friends," the Wizard said, "you have a long journey ahead of you to return to your homes. I shall summon the bats to lead you safely out of the cave. There may still be dangers ahead before this quest is complete. Be wise and be careful." He looked directly at Carling. "I will visit you again."

"But what of Shim? What will become of him?" asked Carling.

Vidente looked over at the Tommy Knocker. "Oh, don't worry about him. He'll be fine. He just needs to stay where he is until you are out of the cave."

"You and that Stone of Mercy," Tandum said to Carling. "I wonder what the Stone of Courage will do to you."

The Wizard nodded and smiled. "Yes, both are important virtues for a leader." With that, the Wizard of Crystonia disappeared, leaving only a dozen twinkling stars to glimmer and fall to the moss-covered floor.

CHAPTER 11

The Ogres

SOON AFTER THE WIZARD disappeared, the low rumble of the bats' flapping wings was heard coming from one of the many tunnels that opened off the cavern. It grew quickly in volume until the bats arrived, filling the great grotto.

The journey out of the cave was long and hard. The tunnels they traveled were not lit by the orange glowing stones found elsewhere in the cave. Their only light was from the two softly glowing stones Carling and Higson had picked up earlier. The bats, not encumbered by the darkness, had a tendency to fly faster than the Centaurs, who were carrying the Duende, could walk. Even with four legs to keep them upright, Tibbals and Tandum stumbled frequently on the rough, dark pathways of the cave. When the bats got out of sight, the Centaurs had no choice but to stop and wait for them to come back and get them.

The route back was a different one than the route Carling and Higson had taken, fortunately. Carling was relieved about this as she didn't know how Tibbals and

Tandum would have done leaping from one small column to another. But most of this tunnel was a long, steep, uphill climb. Soon, the physical exertion coupled with the heat resulted in the young Centaurs sweating profusely. On top of that, all four travelers were nearly overcome with hunger and thirst.

Finally, a dim light appeared ahead. "I see the end," Tibbals said with a squeal. "Thank goodness! I wasn't sure I could take one more step."

Carling swung down from Tibbals's back and walked out of the cave. The cool night air greeted her like an old friend. Above, the night stars twinkled like jewels and the full moon painted everything silver. Carling breathed in deeply, appreciating the sweet smell of the fresh air. She turned around, her arms outstretched. "We made it!" she said, smiling broadly.

Tibbals and Tandum stepped out of the cave. Higson dropped to the ground from Tandum's back. "I'd like to suggest we never return to this horrible cave."

"I couldn't agree more," added Tandum.

Tibbals twisted her hair into a bun on the top of her head and let the cool air bathe her neck. Looking up at the night sky, she said, "For a while there, I wasn't sure if I'd ever see stars again."

"Let's find a place to sleep for the night," suggested Carling.

"How about some water first?" proposed Tandum.

"I remember seeing a stream at the base of this cliff," said Higson.

All four companions, desperately in need of water, started down the narrow trail that traversed the side of the cliff.

The trail along the cliff was as treacherous going down as it had been going up, perhaps more so due to the darkness. Each Duende foot and Centaur hoof had to be carefully placed to keep from slipping on a loose rock. But the thought of water kept them moving, and they finally found themselves at the base of the cliff. Here the trees concealed what little light the moon had to offer, but the travelers easily found the little stream by following the sound of water gurgling as it bounced over rocks.

Carling dropped to her knees at the edge of the stream, cupped her hands, and filled them with water. Handful after handful, she gulped down the ice-cold water. It seemed like she would never get enough.

Tibbals folded her front legs and kneeled down beside Carling. "Your face is so dirty and your hair is messy. Let me help you get cleaned up," she said kindly. With a soft cloth from her bag, she rubbed Carling's nose and cheeks. With a comb, she gently untangled her curls. Carling smiled to herself. If asked, she would have to admit she hadn't even given her appearance a thought. Leave it to Tibbals to keep her looking like a girl.

Tibbals leaned back. "There! That's much better. I wouldn't say you exactly look like a queen, but at least you don't look like a street rat."

"Did I look like a street rat?" Carling asked with a laugh.

"Pretty much!"

The two girls giggled and hugged. Carling felt gratitude for this wonderful, loyal friend filling her heart. "You're the best, Tibbals," she whispered.

Most of the food and provisions they brought with them had been lost in the cave. Only Tibbals had managed to keep her bag strapped to her back, but it was filled mainly with grooming items. The only other possessions they still had were their weapons. At least for this they were thankful.

But one can't eat swords or arrows and it was too dark to hunt in the forest or fish in the stream. They were simply going to have to go to sleep on empty stomachs if they were able.

They snuggled up next to one another on a patch of ground, pine needles providing the only padding. Carling wrapped Tibbals's long tail around her for some warmth. It helped a bit. Hungry, cold, and uncomfortable, the four adventurers suffered through a very long night in the Northern Reaches.

Carling awoke suddenly, not sure what had pulled her from her dreams. The sun was shining brightly, casting shadows from the jagged peaks that surrounded them. Frost covered the ground and the pine needles overhead were painted in glistening white. The air smelled fresh and clean. Just as she pushed her arms skyward to stretch the soreness out of her body, something hard hit her on the head.

"Ouch," she said.

Sitting on the ground next to her was a pinecone. She sat up and looked into the tree branches. A large brown squirrel stared down at her with his beady black eyes. His mouth was pulled up in what could best be described as a grin...if squirrels can grin. As she watched, he dropped another pinecone, this time hitting Higson.

"Hey!" shouted Higson as he opened his eyes and looked around in surprise.

At that moment, dozens of pinecones began showering down upon them. Tibbals squealed and covered her face with her hands. Tandum grabbed his sword, jumped up, reared on his hind legs, and began swinging the sword widely in the air. "Get away! Get away, you little monsters," he shouted.

The squirrels chattered gaily, not the least bit frightened.

Whizz! An arrow sailed through the air and found its mark, causing one of the squirrels to fall to the ground. The rest scattered like leaves before a storm.

Higson walked over to the fallen squirrel, pulled out his arrow, and picked up the dead animal. "Breakfast, anyone?" he said with a mischievous grin.

Squirrel meat never tasted so good!

By the time the sun was high in the sky, the travelers started working their way to the south. They had Mount Heilodius as a landmark, but that didn't help when it came to figuring out all the twists and turns the trails took between the peaks and valleys of the Northern Reaches. They often worked their way between two mountain ridges only to come to a dead end and be forced to turn back.

"I wish we had marked our trail when the Ice Horses were leading us," said Tibbals with a sigh. "I could have used some of my hair ribbons and tied them to trees."

Carling nodded, not surprised that Tibbals had brought along hair ribbons. "That would have been a good idea," she said. "Too bad we didn't think of it." They turned around and searched for yet another route that would take them south.

It was late in the afternoon when they crossed a large stream and started working their way between two steep, rock-strewn hillsides. Carling felt the hair on the back of her neck rise and an involuntary shiver flow through her body. Tibbals must have felt it for she asked, "Are you okay?"

"I don't know. I just have the uncomfortable feeling we're being watched."

Tibbals stopped and looked around. "I don't see anything."

"I guess it's just my imagination," Carling said. But her senses remained on high alert. Every whisper of the breeze, every crack of a twig caused her to jump.

"Relax, Carling. We're fine," said Tibbals.

But just as she said this, a massive chunk of rock broke away from the hillside on their right and rolled down the hill. It landing in the middle of the path in front of them. Suddenly, the rock transformed into a giant creature standing on two legs that appeared to be made of stone. From the large torso, two thick arms unfolded and dropped nearly to the ground. The creature was hunched over, glaring at them through cold, black eyes that looked to be made of coal. The monster's head was square and hairless. Its nose and jaw appeared to be chiseled from stone. Its mouth hung open, and long streams of drool fell to the ground and pooled on the rough surface of the trail.

Tibbals screamed. Tandum reared up on his hind legs, nearly unseating Higson, who had to grab onto the Centaur's shoulders to stay on. "Ogre," Tandum said, his voice shaking.

Instantly, several more massive stones rolled down the hill and reshaped themselves into the same ugly stone creatures as the first.

They formed a wall across the path, blocking their way. The first Ogre growled. When he spoke, his voice sounded like rocks crashing together. "Who are you and what are you doing in our land?"

Carling felt the Stone of Courage burn into her chest. She was surprised at the sudden feeling of bravery that flowed through her. She swung her right leg over Tibbals's back and slid down to the ground. Even with her heart pounding and her mind a jumble of thoughts, she felt a strange sense of confidence. The young girl stepped forward, her chin high, her shoulders back.

Carling stopped a short distance away from the Ogres. She slowly lifted her eyes, up, up, up until she was looking into the face of one of the stone monsters. She suddenly realized how very small she was. She swallowed. Her voice quivered slightly as she started to speak.

"I am Carling from the village of Duenton. These are my friends: Higson, also from my village, and Tibbals and Tandum from the city of Minsheen. We have journeyed to your land, the Northern Reaches, on assignment from Vidente, the Wizard of Crystonia."

"Vidente sent you?" one of the Ogres said with a grumble. More drool dripped from all their mouths and puddled at their stone feet. "Why would the great Wizard of Crystonia do that?"

"We were sent to collect a stone he had left with Shim."

"Ha! Now I know you are lying. No one would entrust anything to that vile creature, let alone a great wizard like Vidente."

Higson dismounted and stepped up beside Carling. "What she is telling you is the truth."

A few of the Ogres snorted in derision. "If this is the truth, show us the stone," said one.

Carling looked at Higson, then back at the Centaurs. She wasn't sure what she should do. Tibbals gave a slight shake of her head as if to tell her "no."

Carling turned back around. "Vidente has not given me permission to show anyone the stone. I'm sure you can respect that. All we ask is that we be allowed to complete our journey back to our homes. We do not desire to disturb you in any way."

"Well, you already have," shouted one.

Just as Carling feared this was not going to end well, the first Ogre that had rolled down the mountain raised his long arms. Looking back and forth at his companions, he smiled a stiff, awkward smile. "I can see they mean us no harm. Let us help them on their way."

The other Ogres mumbled back and forth but eventually agreed.

"We will lead you in the right direction," said the first Ogre. All the Ogres turned to lead the way down the path. Carling, Higson, and the Centaurs hesitantly followed. But Carling couldn't erase the doubt and worry that filled her heart. Something just didn't feel right, though she couldn't say exactly what was wrong. Since they seemed to be moving in the right direction, she continued to follow the Ogres.

After a long walk, the Ogres stopped at the edge of a deep gorge. Spanning the canyon was a narrow suspension bridge. The strong breeze coming up from the base of the gorge swung the bridge from side to side. Carling looked over the edge and into the gorge. Several hundred feet below was a wild river, the architect of the canyon. She swallowed hard and sat back upright.

The Ogres turned and faced Carling and her companions. Motioning toward the bridge, their leader said, "Just cross this bridge and follow the trail to the right. It is a shortcut around Mound Heilodius. You will be home in no time." His stony face broke into a straight smile and drool hung from the corners of his mouth.

"I was afraid he was going to say that," whispered Tibbals.

Carling patted Tibbals on the back and then looked up at the Ogres. "Thank you so much," she said, ashamed that she had doubted their intentions.

Carling and Higson dismounted and Carling led the way onto the bridge. There were ropes on both sides for them to hold as they crossed. The boards had gaps between them, but each board was wide enough for the Centaurs' hooves. The bridge bounced wildly as each new member of their party stepped onto it. Carling gripped the side rope tightly and slowly made her way forward.

Tibbals and Tandum had the advantage of four hooves to balance on but still needed to hold tightly to the side ropes with their hands.

Tibbals swished her tail in anxiety and refused to look down. "I hate heights," she whispered between clenched teeth.

"You're okay. I'm right behind you," said Tandum.

They were in the middle of the bridge and Carling was feeling a little more comfortable as she started to work her way up the second half when she chanced to look back. She gasped. Standing at the beginning of the bridge, the Ogres were sawing at the ropes that held the bridge. "Hold on to the ropes!" cried Carling.

Before she had a chance to explain, one set of ropes gave way and the bridge tipped wildly to one side. Carling and Tibbals screamed as their feet slipped off the boards. Then the other side gave way, and the entire bridge dropped and swung toward the cliff on the far side of the gorge, carrying its cargo with it.

CHAPTER 12

Climbing to Safety

THEY HIT THE SIDE of the cliff hard, but everyone held on. The Centaurs had the hardest time as their horse-like bodies each weighed nearly a thousand pounds. Strong as they were, their arms couldn't hold that much weight for long. Tibbals and Tandum struggled to secure their front and back hooves in gaps between the boards to relieve the strain on their arms. Carling and Higson did the same with their feet. Clutching the ropes, they all held on to the now-vertical bridge, trying to catch their breaths and their wits.

Carling looked back across the ravine. The Ogres were buckled over with laughter. She closed her eyes, trying to get control of the fury she felt inside. She couldn't afford to waste any energy on anger. She looked up. It was still quite a long way to the top of the cliff. The sides of the rock were too smooth to climb, something the Centaurs would never be able to do anyway. There were no trees or bushes to which she could cling if she let go of the bridge. She looked down. It was even farther to the bottom, where she could hear the crashing of the river over rocks. The way she saw it, they had only one choice...start climbing up the bridge.

"Is everyone in one piece?" she asked.

Tibbals whimpered but couldn't speak. The boys said they were alive but did not sound happy.

"Take one of the dangling ropes and tie it around your waist," Carling suggested. Tibbals was afraid to let go even with one hand, so Higson maneuvered down the dangling bridge and tied a rope around her body and secured it behind her front legs.

Once everyone had a safety rope around them, Carling started climbing up the boards on the bridge as though they were a ladder. She and Higson were adept at it. Tibbals and Tandum, not so much. The Centaurs grasped the boards with their hands, but their hooves often slipped off. Lifting one hoof at a time, they slowly worked their way up the makeshift ladder behind the two Duende.

As she climbed, Carling became aware that her ankle was hurting badly. Each time she put her weight on that foot, she nearly cried out in pain. The crash against the cliff must have caused a more severe injury than she'd realized at the time. Now it was letting her know something was wrong. Nevertheless, she kept climbing. Each step on a new board was a fight against her unruly body, a fight she refused to lose. Each step brought excruciating pain. She opened her mouth and started panting, trying to keep her focus on the next board and not think about the pain. Finally, she had to stop and rest.

"Carling, what can I do to help you?" Higson asked from just below her.

She took in a deep, shuddering breath. "Nothing...just need...a rest...I'm okay."

"No, you are *not* okay. Your leg is bleeding all over me!"

Carling tried to look down but immediately was struck with a wave of vertigo. She turned back and looked up to the top of the cliff. It wasn't much farther. "I'm sorry about the blood. But...really...I'll be okay...just need to get to the top."

Gritting her teeth, she started climbing again.

CHAPTER 13

Back in the City of Minsheen

CARLING CROUCHED DOWN, HER heart pounding wildly in her chest. Surrounding her on all sides, Ogres were moving toward her, their stony faces either grinning or smirking. Drool fell in great shimmering sheets from the corners of their mouths. Closer and closer they came. She looked frantically from side to side, searching for a way to escape. Still the Ogres drew nearer and nearer. She heard their gravelly voices taunting her.

"Thought you could get away, did you?"

"Can't outsmart us so easily, can you?"

"So, you thought you were so brave you could stand up to us!"

Brave? The Stone of Courage! Carling's hands flew to her chest. Gone! The silver breastplate was gone! Carling pulled her tunic over her head and waited for the inevitable.

"Carling. Carling, wake up."

She felt the tunic being pulled back off her head. A bright light assaulted her eyes as she struggled to open them. At last, her surroundings came into focus. She wasn't surrounded by Ogres at all. She was in a white room, lying on a soft white bed. The sheet that covered her head had been pulled back by Tibbals. Smiling down at her were Tibbals and Tandum, and beside her was Higson.

Carling blinked and shook her head. "Where am I?" she asked, scratching her cheek and waiting for her heart to slow down.

Tibbals giggled. "You're in the healing rooms in the city of Minsheen."

"Minsheen? But the Ogres? The cliff? The...the bridge?"

"You made it to the top, Carling," said Higson as he reached out and clutched her hand. "You helped us all get to the top. Had it not been for you and your bravery, we all would have died."

"My bravery? I was a fool to think I could trust the Ogres!"

"Not true," said Tandum. "My father said the Ogres would probably have made a feast of us if you hadn't stood up to them."

Higson chuckled. "We're supposed to think we were lucky they just tried to kill us."

Carling shook her head and blinked. Her mouth opened, but nothing came out.

Tibbals giggled again. "You're probably wondering how you got here."

Carling nodded and clamped her mouth shut.

"After you pulled all of us to the top of the cliff, you fainted dead away. In fact, we feared you had died, you'd lost so much blood after all."

"Tandum carried you for two days until we reached the city of Minsheen," said Higson.

Carling's eyes widened. "Two days? How long was I unconscious?"

"Oh, that was almost five days ago," said Higson.

"We brought you to the city healer, Chamay. She gave you something to help you sleep while she worked on your broken leg. We've been waiting for you to wake up ever since," explained Tandum with a smile.

Carling had completely forgotten about her injury. "My leg was broken?" she asked, lifting her head and looking down.

Tibbals pulled back the white blanket to reveal a band wrapped around her left leg. "Don't worry. Chamay has you all fixed up. You'll be as good as new in no time."

At that moment, a white Centaur entered the room. She was dressed in a white cloak that buttoned up the front. Her skin was pale and her hair, which was tied in a tight bun at the nape of her neck, was as white as her body and tail. She wore a tiny white cap on the top of her head. The only thing that wasn't white about her were her plump, rosy cheeks and her dark brown eyes.

"Did I hear my name?" she asked in a high, flowery voice.

Her eyes went to the patient in the bed. "My, my. So you're finally awake, are you? I'm so glad. I'm afraid I'm much more accustomed to treating Centaurs with our big bodies. Never treated a little Duende before," she said as she laughed lightheartedly. "I'm afraid I gave you a bit too much potion. You had me worried there for a bit. Of course you'd have had one of your own to blame. Got it from the famous Duende healer, Pernilla Persdotter."

Carling cocked her head and raised her eyebrows. She had never heard of Pernilla Persdotter.

"Oh, you don't know her?" asked Chamay, clearly reading Carling's expression. "She has a wonderful apothecary in the village of Madiera on the shores of the Swirling Sea. Wonderful, talented woman she is. Get many of my potions from her."

Carling felt herself getting tired and weak. She laid back and closed her eyes.

Chamay recognized the signs. "Okay, everyone," she said. "Shoo, shoo. My patient needs her rest. You can come back tomorrow."

Tibbals bent down and kissed Carling on the forehead. Higson gave her hand a squeeze. Tandum tapped her good foot. And then Chamay literally pushed them out of the room.

When her friends had left, Carling wrapped her arms around her body. Then she gasped. "My breastplate! My breastplate is gone!"

She looked from side to side. There was no sign of it. "Chamay! Chamay!" she called out.

She heard the soft clip-clop sound of hooves on the smooth stone floor. The white Centaur returned to her room. "You called me?"

"Chamay, the Silver Breastplate. It's gone."

"Do not worry your pretty little head. I've put it in a safe place."

"You took it off me? It didn't hurt you?" asked Carling, remembering how the shield had shocked the Heilodius Centaurs who tried to grab her at Fort

Heilodius. And the Bat that tried to attack her had fallen dead away. They had been unable to touch her. She made a mental note to ask the Wizard about that the next time she saw him.

"Heaven's no. Why would it?" The nurse walked across the room, bent down and opened a cupboard door. Then Chamay pulled out a bundle wrapped with a white blanket.

Carling watched as she carefully unwrapped the blanket, revealing her beautiful Silver Breastplate. The young Duende released a long sigh of relief. "Thank you for taking care of it."

Chamay approached the bed, carrying the breastplate. "Carling, I need to ask you something. Perhaps it's none of my business...no, I'm quite sure it's none of my business...but..."

"Go ahead. Ask me," Carling said.

"Well, I was just wondering if...if perhaps...this could possibly be the eminent and long-awaited Silver Breastplate about which legends have been told."

Carling nodded her head. "Yes, Chamay. It is the Silver Breastplate whose wearer is heir to the throne of Crystonia."

Chamay gasped. "But when your friends brought you in, you were wearing it."

Carling nodded again.

"Am I to conclude, then, that you are to be our future queen? Can this be?"

"You can't be more surprised than I, Chamay," said Carling as she glanced away from the healer.

"Do Tibbals and Tandum know about this?"

"Yes. They have been sent to accompany me as I gather the stones and complete the breastplate."

"Does Manti know about it?"

Carling shook her head. "I don't think so."

"But he should, don't you think? He *is* the leader of the Minsheen herd after all."

"The Wizard, Vidente, who gave me the breastplate, told me to tell no one unless he first gave me permission."

"I see. Well, I will honor that and tell no one, either. However, since you are now in Manti's care and his children have been helping you, perhaps you could ask the Wizard for permission to tell him."

Carling nodded. "I will do so as soon as he appears."

"And when will that be?"

Carling shrugged. "I never know. He just comes and goes." Suddenly a thought entered her head. "Chamay, the Commander of the Heilodius Herd knows about it."

The healer's eyes opened wide. "That changes things. Now I believe you owe it to Manti to tell him. And the sooner, the better!"

CHAPTER 14

The Feast

A FEW DAYS LATER, Carling was moved into her own room. It was the most magnificent bedroom she had ever seen. The walls sparkled with a plaster that must have been embedded with tiny jewels. Paintings of Centaurs adorned the walls. Two tall windows faced to the east and were draped with golden curtains. Fresh summer flowers arranged in a vase on a dresser filled the room with their sweet aroma. In the center was a bed built for a Centaur. It was so big Carling was sure she would get lost in it. But the very best part was that Tibbals was right next door.

Carling's left leg was healing quickly, and she could gingerly walk on it now without help. However, a slow, lopsided walk was all she could manage, so she still spent most of her time on her big bed. Tibbals kept her entertained by reading stories from Centaur books with titles such as "A Series of Unfortunate Centaurs," "Little Fillies," and her favorite, "In the Heart of a Centaur." They played Tibbals's favorite board game, "Centopoly," over and over.

Higson and Tandum continued to improve their sword-brandishing skills in the courtyard beneath Carling's window. The sounds of the swords clashing floated up through the open window and gave her a strange sense of comfort.

One day, just as the summer sun was starting to send its warmth and light through the windows, Tibbals rushed into her friend's room. "Carling! Carling, are you feeling better today?"

Carling stretched and rolled over. "I think so. It's too early to tell." Carling had become accustomed to sleeping longer than usual, probably the result of the potions Chamay continued to give her.

"Daddy is hosting a feast tonight. I want you to come!"

"A feast? What's the occasion?"

"I don't know. It's all been very hush-hush. Something to do with the meetings he's been having."

"Meetings with whom?

"I don't know that, either." Tibbals swished her long, blond tail from side to side. "But it doesn't matter. Any excuse for a banquet is fine with me." Then her hand flew to her mouth. "My goodness, look at you. We have so much work to do!"

Over the next several hours, Tibbals was in her element. Carling was bathed in bubbles and then covered with perfume, her hair washed and scented. Tibbals went through every item of clothing she owned to find just the right garment for Carling. Tibbals's dresses, made just long enough to cover the human-like part of her body, were long on Carling. Tibbals described them as "elegant." The Centaur filly decided green was the best color to go with Carling's auburn curls and violet eyes, so all other options were cast aside.

Jewelry was next. Tibbals, as was to be expected, had quite a collection of valuable baubles. "Purple stones match your eyes and really stand out on the green fabric, don't you think?" said Tibbals, who was really having way too much fun treating Carling like a dress-up doll.

Carling nodded. She had never had the luxury of playing dress-up and wasn't completely comfortable doing so now. But any time spent with Tibbals was always fun, so she played along.

By the time the gong was struck, announcing that the time to enter the dining room had arrived, Carling was finished to Tibbals's satisfaction. The Centaur stepped back. "You look ravishing. You look like a...a queen!" she said, tears suddenly flowing down her cheeks.

Carling reached up and hugged her friend.

Carling didn't feel much like a queen as she limped down the wide staircase built to accommodate four-legged Centaurs. Each tread was so long she had to take three or four steps on each one. She grasped the carved, wooden handrail tightly as she lowered her foot down each step so as not to fall.

But the reaction to her appearance as she descended told her that Tibbals had succeeded in her mission to make her look beautiful.

When she reached the bottom of the long staircase, Higson rushed up to her and offered her his arm. Grinning broadly, he said, "May I escort you, my lady?"

Carling heard Tibbals giggle behind her. She turned back and gave the filly her best scowl.

Side by side, the little Duende entered the great hall where the feast was set and ready. They were so short they could see little beyond the hundreds of Centaur legs milling around the room. Looking up, Carling noticed elegant lanterns hanging from the ceiling, their candles casting a warm light over the guests and tables. The walls were lined with silver candelabras that each held a dozen more candles. The tables were set with elegant china and crystal and decorated with massive bouquets of flowers. Pulled up to the long tables were the padded and upholstered benches preferred by the Centaurs. Carling and Higson shared one of these as Tibbals and Tandum folded their legs and made themselves comfortable on benches set on either side of the young Duende.

Carling looked over at Tibbals and smiled. Her dear friend, not surprisingly, looked gorgeous. Her nearly white blond hair was braided with flowers and ribbons, and the rose-colored blouse that covered her human-like torso reflected the pink in her cheeks.

Carling wasn't the only one who noticed how beautiful the filly looked. It seemed every Centaur colt in the enormous room made his way past her bench to say hello. Tibbals's hand must have been kissed by several dozen young colts before the dinner even began.

Of course, Tandum was getting his share of flirtatious glances from the fillies in the room. It seemed that only the older Centaurs acknowledged Carling and Higson with words of welcome. This was fine with Carling.

Two Centaurs with trumpets entered the room through the tall golden entry doors, prompting a hush to fall over the crowd. The two Centaurs then raised their trumpets and blew a fanfare. All heads turned.

"Father and Mother are coming," said Tibbals, excitement in her voice.

While the Centaurs stood, Carling climbed up on her bench to see Manti and the lead mare of the herd, Tamah, enter the room. Suddenly, a cold fear gripped her heart just as Tibbals gripped her hand. "Carling, look!" she heard Tibbals hiss.

Walking in behind Manti was a very large Centaur dressed in a black shirt as worn by all the Heilodius herd. However, this shirt was adorned with a silver crown encircled by stars...this was the Commander. Carling recognized him immediately as the Centaur who had imprisoned Tibbals, Tandum, Higson, and her in the dungeon of Fort Heilodius. She was staring at him, her mouth gaping, when he turned and locked eyes with her. A sardonic grin crossed his face as he winked. Carling sucked in a quick breath, clamped her mouth shut, and sat down quickly on her bench. Stunned by the sudden appearance of the Commander, in the city of Minsheen of all places, Carling realized she had suddenly lost her appetite.

"Tibbals," she whispered, "what is the Commander doing here?"

"I can't imagine," Tibbals responded, clearly as confused as Carling. "I don't understand it. What is my father thinking?"

Once the crowd returned to their seats, Carling could see the Commander sitting at the head table right next to Manti. When he stared at her once again, she quickly looked away.

While Carling noticed that several of the Centaurs pointed at the Commander and whispered to one another, their apparent concern did not last long. Soon, happy chatter filled the room.

"Why would my father invite him here?" Tandum asked under his breath.

"Do you think he's been meeting with the Commander secretly the last few days?" whispered Tibbals.

"What do you know about those meetings?" asked Higson.

"Every time I tried to meet with Father," Tandum said, "Mother said he was tied up in a conference. She wouldn't tell me who he was meeting with or what it was about. I thought it all very strange at the time. But now this..." Tandum frowned and glanced up at the head table. The Commander was watching the four of them. Tandum looked quickly away.

Centaurs dressed in black and white outfits circled the room, bringing great platters of colorful foods. They served each guest until their silver plates were piled high. Carling picked at her food, mainly just pushing it around on her plate. She tried to listen to the beautiful music being performed by a quartet of four Centaurs, three playing violins and one a harp. Usually music could calm her troubled soul, but not tonight.

After dessert was served and eagerly consumed by most in the room, Manti arose from his bench and tapped his goblet with a silver fork. "Attention! Attention! May I have everyone's attention, please."

The guests immediately stopped their chatter. The quartet stopped their playing. All eyes turned to face the esteemed leader of the herd.

"I want to thank all of you for attending the celebration tonight...for a celebration it is. You will notice that on my right hand sits my brother and yours, the Commander of the Heilodius herd."

Murmuring was heard throughout the hall. Manti tapped his goblet again and all was quiet.

"As you all know, relations between our two herds have been strained for quite some time." More murmuring was heard. Manti held up a hand. "Yes, yes...perhaps I did not choose my words correctly. Let me begin again. For some time, there has been a great division in the proud race of Centaurs...a division that most felt could never be healed. Our vision for the future of the Land of Crystonia has been very different from that of the Heilodius herd." Manti paused and looked around the room, a smile on his face, his eyes twinkling beneath his wavy gray hair. He continued. "Well, I am pleased to announce that, from this night onward, the Centaurs are once again united."

A loud clap of thunder followed by a bright flash of lightning rattled the windows that ran the length of one side of the chamber, causing all the guests to jump in their seats. Carling felt her heart pounding in her chest as she waited to hear what else Manti had to say.

Manti cleared his throat and began again. "My brother, the Commander of the Heilodius herd, and I have been meeting over the last several days to work out our differences. I won't lie to you. It wasn't always a pleasant experience," he said, turning to give his brother a warm smile. "But, after much discussion and debate, we have decided, for the good of all Centaurs everywhere, to settle our differences and reunite as a single herd."

A stunned silence fell over the entire room. This was followed by a din of confusion.

Manti raised his hands for silence. "Yes, yes. I'm sure there are many questions. We have anticipated such. I will try to answer them all. First, I'm sure you are wondering who will govern our race. The Commander and I will be co-governors. We will rule from the city of Minsheen. There will still be a Centaur army, as there are forces in the land that are seeking to rule Crystonia and all its inhabitants. We need to be able to protect ourselves if we are attacked. However, we have agreed that we will not be the aggressors. Our army will be trained at Fort Heilodius, and the Commander will continue to spend most of his time overseeing their progress."

The Centaurs around the room began whispering back and forth to one another.

Manti lifted a silver goblet. "Let us toast to our renewed unity."

Quietly and hesitantly, Centaurs throughout the hall lifted their cups in unison with Manti. Carling, Higson, Tibbals, and Tandum did not.

After the announcement, guests remained in the great hall, milling around and talking with one another in hushed voices as the string quartet resumed playing.

Carling, Higson, Tibbals, and Tandum worked their way between the clusters of Centaurs toward the great golden doors, trying to exit as quickly as they could without running. But they weren't fast enough.

Suddenly, the Commander appeared right in front of them, blocking their exit. "Did you enjoy the festivities?" he asked with a sneer.

"Yes, thank you," they lied.

"I really wish you wouldn't rush off. I'm curious to know what you think of our new...er...*arrangement*," he said, his black tail swishing and his black eyes narrowing. He drummed his fingers on his chest and waited for a response as he kept his eyes on Carling.

"I think anything that helps bring peace to the land is wonderful news for us all," she said, raising her chin to look the Commander directly in the eyes. "I only hope this is not some sort of trick on your part."

The Commander's eyes opened wide and a smile danced across his face. "A trick? Why, my dear Carling, your words pierce me to my heart. Can you possibly be questioning my motivation?"

Carling raised her eyebrows. "Yes, Commander, I am."

CHAPTER 15

Spies

"NO, I WON'T HEAR of it," said Chamay sharply. "You are much too weak. You must stay here where I can take care of you."

The Centaur healer was standing in Carling's room, responding to the young Duende's request to return to her village of Duenton. Since the feast, Carling had been filled with a strong desire to check on her villagers to make sure they were safe. She didn't trust the Commander and wondered if he had done anything to harm the village of Duenton in her absence.

"Chamay," she said, "I promise to return in just a few days. I just want to check on my village."

"The journey would be too hard on your leg. It is still too fragile."

"Look," said Carling as she stood up from the chair in which she had been lounging. "I can walk on it really well." She clenched her teeth and did her best to walk around without showing any sign of a limp.

Chamay wasn't fooled.

"If I must," she said, "I will contact Manti and he will order you to remain."

Carling shook her head and sat back down. "That won't be necessary," she said with a sigh.

"Good. I'm glad I was able to talk some sense into that lovely head of yours." Chamay turned and with a swish of her white tail left the room, her hooves clipping and clopping on the floor. Carling listened as the sound of her healer's hooves receded then sat back in her chair, discouraged.

As soon as Chamay left, Higson came into Carling's room. "You're looking rather down," he said. "What's the matter?"

"Chamay won't let me go to the village to check on our people."

"Are you worried about them?"

"Well, *of course* I'm worried about them. Aren't you?"

Higson, who apparently hadn't thought much about the villagers of Duenton, scratched his head. "I *suppose* we should be. I've just been having too much fun in Minsheen."

"Higson!"

"Sorry, but it's true. Tandum has some really fun friends."

"Well, we have more important things to do than just play games."

Higson frowned. "You used to be so much fun."

Carling lowered her chin to her chest. "I know. I haven't been much fun for a long time. I'm sorry."

"No," said Higson, contrite. "*I'm* sorry. I shouldn't have said that. You've been given a huge responsibility, and I'm sure it's a burden that is hard for you to carry.

Speaking of responsibility, have you had a visit from the Wizard lately?"

Carling shook her head. "No, and I wish he would return to tell me what to do about the Commander. He seems to like to let me struggle."

"I have an idea about the Commander," said Higson with a twinkle in his eyes.

"You do? What's your idea?" asked Carling, sitting up and leaning toward him, her eyes wide with anticipation.

"I say we spy on him."

"Spy?"

"Yes. The four of us can divide up in pairs and keep a lookout on what he's doing and where he's going."

"That doesn't sound so easy."

"I didn't say it would be easy."

Carling ran her fingers through her auburn curls and pursed her lips. "Let's talk this over with Tibbals and Tandum. Tibbals said they would both stop by."

Tibbals and Tandum arrived in Carling's room a short time later.

"How is your leg doing?" Tibbals asked as she cradled Carling's face between her cupped hands.

Carling smiled. "It's much better. Chamay isn't convinced, however. She won't let me go to Duenton."

"Why do you need to go to your village?" asked Tandum.

"I'm just worried about everyone there. I assume they are safe, but I hate not knowing."

"I will go and check on things there. Then I'll return and report to you," said Tandum.

"You'd do that?" Carling said, her smile broad, her eyes sparkling as she looked at her friend. "Oh, Tandum, thank you!"

Higson joined in. "I'll go with him," he said, perhaps a bit jealous of the appreciation being given to Tandum.

Higson climbed on Tandum's back. "We'll be back before the sun sets," Tandum said. They dashed out of the room, leaving Tibbals to spoil Carling. For the moment, Carling forgot all about Higson's idea to spy on the Commander.

Tandum and Higson returned just as the sun was sending long shadows across the sparkling buildings of Minsheen. Their report put Carling's mind at ease. All seemed to be well in Duenton. The Fauns were diligent in their role as guardians in the watchtowers. The villagers were busy with their planting and other tasks. The children were in school. All seemed perfectly normal. Carling breathed a sigh of relief and laid back against the fluffy pillows on her bed.

Tandum, who had cantered all the way to Duenton and back, was weary. After making his report, he retired to his room.

Tibbals and Higson remained with Carling.

Her mind at ease at last, Carling thought about the Commander again. "Higson," she said, "what was your idea about keeping watch on the Commander?"

Tibbals cocked her head and waited for Higson to speak.

"While you've been recuperating," Higson said, "things have been happening in Minsheen that I don't like."

"I don't like them, either," said Tibbals. "Have you seen how many Heilodius soldiers are in the city? It's creepy."

"Yes. And they're posted everywhere."

"What are they doing here?" asked Carling.

"I don't know. Father said they're supposed to be protecting us, but it feels more like they're spying on us," said Tibbals. "I feel like a prisoner in my own city."

"I'm quite sure they're infiltrating the city," said Higson, his eyebrows knotted with concern. "That's why I think we need to start keeping an eye on the Commander."

The three friends stayed up late into the night discussing Higson's plan. In the morning, they brought Tandum on board.

"You're right, Higson," the Centaur colt said. "Things are not good. We need to figure out what's going on."

"I'm surprised a wise Centaur such as your father wouldn't be more aware of this," said Carling as she adjusted her injured leg on a pillow.

"I've been wondering about that myself," said Higson.

"I think Father is just so eager to mend the damage to his relationship with his brother he's blind to what might be going on," said Tibbals. "He doesn't want to think the Commander, his own brother, is double-crossing him."

Carling nodded in understanding.

For the next several days, Tibbals, Tandum, Higson, and Carling placed themselves as close as possible to the Commander's rooms. Tibbals dressed like one of the cleaning mares and used a feather duster to repeatedly clean the portraits of famous Centaurs that hung on either side of the Commander's door. Tandum, dressed as a maintenance stallion in a white, paint-splattered smock, painted and repainted the walls in the wide hallway.

Secreted just down the hall behind a statue of a rearing Centaur, Higson kept an eye out in both directions. Hiding in a potted plant where the corridor turned a corner, Carling watched and listened.

They carried on their clandestine observation for several days. On the fourth day, they gathered in Tibbals's room. "This isn't working," the filly said as she removed her maid's uniform and shook out the bun in which she had tied her hair.

Carling plopped down on her friend's large bed. "You're right. We haven't even seen the Commander come out of his room. And all of the Heilodius Centaurs that go in and out aren't saying anything."

"I think we need to watch them at night," suggested Tandum.

Tibbals moaned. "Night? I need my beauty sleep."

"Well, as you said, this isn't working," responded her brother.

"What?" snapped Tibbals, prompting her brother to laugh.

"Sorry," he said, "I didn't mean your beauty sleep isn't working. I meant our daytime spying isn't working."

"Oh. Good," the filly said, slapping her brother on the shoulder. "I was going to be mad at you for a minute there."

So it was agreed that after dinner and a short nap, they would all take up their posts again with some necessary changes. "Painters don't paint at night," Higson reminded everyone.

"Nor do maids dust at night," added Carling.

"So how are we going to disguise ourselves?" asked Tibbals.

There was silence in the room for quite a while.

At last Carling had an idea. They all gathered around and, with heads close together, discussed Carling's plan.

CHAPTER 16

Night Surveillance

THE DOORS TO THE Commander's chambers were in the middle of a long hallway. At the far end, the passage stopped at a wall covered with a huge portrait of Manti and his family. Tibbals and Tandum were both quite young when the portrait was painted, but they were very beautiful foals even then.

As the tapered candles in the holders along the walls burned down, sputtered, and died, sending a spiraling snake of smoke up to the ceiling, the hallway was cast into complete darkness.

"It's time," whispered Carling, who was peeking around the large potted plant that had been her hiding place for several days. Behind her, from their positions crouched in a door well, Tibbals, Tandum, and Higson stepped forward, their hooves and feet not making a sound on the highly polished floor.

"Let's go," whispered Carling.

"Are you sure this will work?" asked Tibbals softly.

Carling shook her head. "No. I'm not sure of anything. It seems like this is a plan where a lot could go wrong but, as we discussed, I can't think of anything better."

The little group silently moved down the hallway past the commander's quarters and stopped in front of the large portrait.

Carling stared up at the painting. "Wow, it's bigger than I thought," she exclaimed.

Tandum and Higson carefully lifted the frame off the wall. They wobbled under the weight of the portrait once they had it off the hooks and in their hands. Tibbals gasped as they nearly tipped it over.

"Sh-h-h-h," everyone said at once, making much more noise than Tibbals had with her gasp.

"Have you got it under control?" asked Carling.

Tandum and Higson set their jaws, gritted their teeth, and nodded.

"Okay. Let's move it forward."

Trying their best to slide their hooves and feet silently along the floor, the four of them moved the portrait down the hall toward the Commander's door. They had moved just a few feet when they heard a door open. Higson and Carling jumped behind the portrait. They all held their breath. Two Minsheen Centaurs walked out of the doors across the hall from the Commander's rooms. They were laughing and talking and didn't even look back down the hall. Carling's heart was pounding so loudly she was surprised they didn't hear her. The four collaborators held their spot until the two Centaurs turned a corner and disappeared from sight.

"The coast is clear," whispered Tibbals after peeking around the edge of the picture frame that held the large canvas. Slowly, silently, they continued moving down the hall. They stopped a few feet away from the Commander's doorway and set the frame down. Tibbals pulled a knife from her belt and poked two slits in the canvas, just at eye level for herself and Tandum. They hurried around behind the picture to wait...for what, they knew not.

Carling stepped back to examine their work. She smiled. The portrait effectively blocked the entire hall, making it look like the passage was twenty tail-lengths (the Centaurs' favorite unit of measure) shorter. It looked, in the darkness of night, like the hall actually ended there.

With Tibbals and Tandum hiding behind the portrait, Carling and Higson moved down the hall to the other side of the Commander's doorway. Carling glanced back and smiled. The portrait was barely visible in the dark hallway, but it did look like the hall was much shorter than it had been before moving the picture. It looked good. Step one had been completed successfully.

The two Duende hurried behind the statue and plant they had used as hiding places during the day. Now, all they could do was wait and see what might come along. Carling folded her lithe body in half and slid to the ground, her back pressed against the wall. She was glad her leg was feeling much stronger and rubbed it gently. After a time, she wiggled around and placed her chin on the top lip of the pot. From this position, she could see any Centaur coming from either direction. She hummed softly to herself, trying to stay awake. But her eyes kept getting heavier and heavier. Time seemed to be moving slowly if, indeed, it was moving at all.

"Higson," she whispered, cupping her hands around her mouth.

No answer.

"Higson," she said again.

No answer.

She crawled out from behind the pot and sneaked up to where Higson was curled up in a ball behind the statue...sound asleep.

"Higson...Higson," she whispered, gently shaking his shoulder.

Higson jerked up. "What? What is it?"

"You fell asleep."

"Oh...sorry."

"I can't say as I blame you. I'm having a hard time staying awake myself. Maybe this was a bad idea," said Carling as she rubbed her eyes.

A few nights later, just as they were about to give up on the whole idea of spying by night, things changed.

Tibbals and Tandum were behind their portrait. Carling and Higson were behind their pot and statue. Carling cupped her hands around her mouth and softly called over to Higson. "Higson, I'm tired of sitting here. Nothing ever happens. Let's give up."

No sooner had she spoken than the door to the Commander's quarters opened with a squeak. A Heilodius Centaur, lit from behind by the glow of candles in the room, poked his head out and looked in both directions. Higson and Carling pressed themselves down to the floor and watched, wide-eyed.

Apparently having seen no one, the Centaur said, "The coast is clear. Let's go." The large, burly Centaur, dressed in the Heilodius herd's black and silver tunic, stepped into the passageway...and was followed by three more of his herdmates.

Carling studied each face. The Commander was not among them. Suddenly, Carling sucked in her breath and began to tremble. In their hands, the Heilodius Centaurs held swords.

As Higson followed the Centaurs from a safe distance around a corner in the passageway, Carling dashed back to confer with Tibbals and Tandum.

"What's going on?" asked Tandum.

"I don't know," Carling said, "but did you see what they were carrying?"

"No," said Tibbals. "It's kind of hard to see through these little slits."

Carling took a deep breath. "They were carrying swords."

Even in the darkness, Carling could see the shocked look on the faces of the brother and sister. Tandum set his jaw then lifted the portrait and placed it against the wall. "Let's go," he said.

Not concerned about silence any longer, Tibbals said, "Get on my back, Carling." The filly lowered a bent knee to the ground and Carling climbed up. Being careful not to slip on the smooth floor, the Centaurs trotted down the hall and around the corner.

As they passed, the door to the Commander's quarters opened slightly. Silent as a shadow, a Centaur stepped out of the doorway and followed the two Centaurs and the little Duende.

CHAPTER 17

Standing Up to the Enemy

TIBBALS, TANDUM, AND CARLING rushed down the passageway and around the corner. At the next junction they looked both ways. They saw no one. Carling looked first one way, then the other, confused as to which way they should go.

"Which way?" she asked, panic evident in her voice.

"The right leads us to the great hall," Tibbals said. "The left goes to Father and Mother's chambers."

Suddenly, Carling saw something on the floor of the passageway leading to the left. She hoped off Tibbals's back, ran up to it, bent down, and picked up a scarf. Holding the scarf up she turned back to Tibbals and Tandum. "This is Higson's. He must have left this so we would know which way they went. Come on. Let's go this way."

"Toward Father and Mother's rooms!" said Tandum, his brow wrinkled. "There's no good reason for them to go this way. We'd better hurry."

Carling swung up on Tibbals's back and the two Centaurs started trotting, making no attempt to move quietly but every attempt to move swiftly.

They were too late.

Rounding the next corner, they heard a scream.

"Mother!" shouted Tibbals.

Tandum started cantering and charged past Higson, who was pressed against a wall, inching forward toward an open door.

Tandum burst through the doorway and slid to a stop, Tibbals and Carling right behind him. Tandum reared up on his hind legs and shouted, "Let go of them!" His eyes flashed with anger.

Carling felt Tibbals's body stiffen beneath her. The young Duende's heart seemed to stop beating as she surveyed the scene that met her eyes.

Standing with arms wrapped around Manti and the lead mare, Tamah, and holding swords pressed against their necks, the four Heilodius Centaurs sneered at the intruders.

"Well, well, well," said one. "What have we here?"

"Release my parents at once," said Tandum, his fists clenched, his eyes narrowed.

"We don't take orders from you, young prince," said another.

Tandum's and Tibbals's mother began to whimper, her face pallid and her eyes blinking rapidly.

"Let her go," said Manti. "It's me you want."

"Oh, I think not," said one of the Centaurs holding Manti. "We've been instructed to bring both of you." He jerked the sword tighter across Manti's neck, causing the stallion to begin choking.

Tandum reared and pawed the air with his front hooves. "Let them go. Now!" he shouted.

Carling grabbed the small knife from Tibbals's belt and leaped off the Centaur's back. Tibbals and Tandum began an attack with the only weapons they had, their hooves. Higson was completely unarmed, and Carling had only the short knife, which was next to worthless considering the size of the opponents and their long swords. But she scurried around the flying legs in an attempt to find an opening.

The Centaurs were dashing around, kicking and rearing, their swords slicing through the air. Carling brought a shaking hand to her forehead and brushed back a damp strand of hair. Beads of sweat formed on her upper lip as her eyes darted from one side of the room to the other, searching for a place to enter the foray successfully. She didn't know what Higson was doing and didn't have time to find out.

"Enough!" a deep voice resonated through the room. "Or our little pest here gets dropped on his ugly head."

Everyone froze in place. As though choreographed, every head turned in the direction from which the sound had come. Framed in the carved doorway was the Commander. One of his strong arms was outstretched in front of him, and in his hand he held Higson by the ankles. The young Duende was flailing wildly, trying to get one of his fists to connect with the Commander's chest.

Manti was the first to speak, a sword still held to his throat. "Brother, what is the meaning of this?"

"What do you think? Did you *actually* believe I was willing to join forces with you and give up on obtaining the throne?"

"I believed you when you said that was your intention, yes."

"Then you're a bigger fool than I've always thought, my dear brother. Thank you for proving me wrong!" the Commander said with a sardonic smile. He turned his head and his eyes narrowed as he looked at Carling. Still speaking to Manti, he said, "Did you really think I would let *you* take control of the throne through your little friend here?"

"Carling?" said Manti, his head flinching back slightly, a blank look on his face. "What does Carling have to do with any of this?"

"Don't tell me you don't know," said the Commander with a sneer.

"Don't know what? Tell me what you're talking about," said Manti.

"Have you been keeping secrets, Carling?" said the Commander, taking a step toward her. "Does Manti really have no idea what you're wearing? I find that very hard to believe since you are in his household."

Carling raised her chin and stepped toward the Commander, the Stone of Courage warm against her chest. "He knows nothing."

"Tsk, tsk. It isn't nice to keep secrets from your host, now, is it?"

"The Wizard did not give me permission to tell him."

"Oh, he didn't? Well, must we do only what the Wizard commands?" The Commander chuckled and looked back and forth at his soldiers. "I don't see a Wizard in our presence, do any of you?"

The soldiers laughed and held their prisoners even tighter.

"I am the Commander and I command you to reveal your secret."

Carling stood her ground, her thoughts a mass of confusion. She didn't know what she should do. She heard Manti's soft, kind voice interrupt the debate raging within her.

"Carling, you must do what you think is right," said Manti kindly.

Feeling a sudden surge of confidence, Carling was sure of what she should do. "I will reveal my secret, Manti."

"Only if you are sure that is the right thing to do...if that is what the Wizard would have you do if he were here."

"I am sure," she said.

Slowly, Carling unwrapped her tunic, revealing the Silver Breastplate. She heard Manti and Tamah gasp.

"Can this be?" said Manti. "The Silver Breastplate of the ruler of Crystonia?"

Carling felt her face flush with color as she nodded, keeping her eyes on the Commander.

"How did you come to possess this?" said the lead stallion.

"The Wizard of Crystonia gave it to me over a year ago."

Manti turned to Tandum and Tibbals, who were standing to one side, their sides still heaving and wet with sweat from their efforts. "Tandum and Tibbals, did you know about this?"

"Yes, Father," they replied in unison.

"Is this where you have been? Is this the secret assignment Adivino gave you?"

They both nodded. "We have been helping Carling complete the shield by gathering the Stones of Light," said Tibbals.

Manti's eyes returned to the shield and examined the stones, noticing the empty spaces. "But I see there are still missing stones."

Carling spoke up. "We have been sent to collect the Stone of Mercy and the Stone of Courage. We know nothing of the other two stones at this time."

Manti turned to the Commander. "And how did you know about this?"

"Your children and the Duende were guests in my fortress."

"Guests? I would call us 'prisoners,'" said Carling.

"You held my foals prisoner?" Tamah nearly shouted. This was met with a jerk from the Centaur who held her tightly.

"Don't harm my mare!" said Manti, glaring at the Heilodius Centaur, fire blazing in his brown eyes. Carling had never seen Manti's eyes look anything but soft and warm.

"I don't see that you can do anything about it," responded the soldier with a growl.

Tandum jumped forward, whirled, and kicked both back legs at the guard. His sharp hooves landed squarely on the soldier's shoulder, creating a deep gash. Blood poured from the wound and down the soldier's leg. The Heilodius Centaur swung his sword toward Tandum. Tandum whirled away from the sharp edge of the blade as it sliced through the air.

"Stop! Stop this instant!" said the Commander, his voice filled with arrogance. He seemed to have forgotten Higson, who still hung from his fist. "I want civility as we discuss our little problem."

"So what is our problem, my brother?" asked Manti, his eyes still flashing with anger. "It appears to me the conflict has been resolved. We all know the one who possesses the Silver Breastplate is the rightful heir to the throne."

"Only if we allow it!" the Commander shouted. He took a deep breath, appearing to try to gain his composure. "Forgive me. I don't want to lose my temper. Now, let us be reasonable. Who, here, really thinks a little Duende girl can rule this land? How is she going to lead the likes of Ogres, Cyclops, and our race, the magnificent and splendid Centaurs? *We* are the ones who are divinely created and uniquely qualified to lead our kingdom, not a weak, miniature creature like *her*!" he said, spinning around to glare at Carling.

He turned back to face Manti. "But I don't blame her. She is just a victim of circumstances. It is really *your* fault," he said, glaring now at his brother, his eyes as cold and hard as coal. "*You* created the void that left the throne empty by not joining me to conquer our enemies."

All eyes were now on Manti as everyone waited for his response. The room was silent. Carling was holding her breath along with everyone else.

Manti stood motionless, but his eyes were still aflame with anger. Carling could see the muscles in his jaw twitching.

Finally he spoke, clearly and slowly enunciating every word. "The rightful heir to the throne has been chosen. It is not ours to take whether by force or by finesse. The young Duende is soon to be our queen. It is our job to sustain and support her."

The expression on the Commander's face became even uglier. "Rubbish!" he shouted. "I and my herd will not be ruled by a Duende, nor by anyone else!" He reared up on his hind legs and pawed the air, then lowered his front hooves with a loud clang that sent sparks flying around the room.

Speaking through clenched teeth, the Commander continued. "So, am I to assume *that* is your final decision, Manti?"

"It is."

"I'm very sorry to hear that. I was hoping we could work together. But I see that is not to be!" Suddenly, the room was filled with a dozen more Heilodius Centaur soldiers. "Take them to the Fort," the Commander shouted.

"All of them?" said one, eyeing Carling and remembering their last encounter with the young Duende when no one could touch her.

"Leave the girl. She is of no use to us."

"And the boy?" asked one, referring to Higson.

The Commander stopped and looked at Higson. He had paid little attention to the young Duende that he still held suspended at arm's length. This other Duende always seemed to be nearby when he encountered Carling. "Let's take him. He might prove to be valuable as a bargaining chip." He dropped Higson to the floor. Higson landed with a thud and scrambled to his feet. He dashed toward Carling but was scooped up by a soldier. "Not so fast, little guy," said the Centaur. "You're coming with me."

"No," shouted Carling. "Leave them and take me. I will go along without resistance."

The Commander glanced over at Carling with a sneer. "Do as I have commanded," he said to his warriors.

The soldiers pushed, prodded, and kicked Manti, Tamah, Tibbals, and Tandum out the doorway. Higson was being carried in the strong arms of a soldier while he yelled and struggled to get free. Carling dashed forward, intent on following, but her path was blocked by the Commander, who now held a sword in each hand, his tail swishing in anger.

"Not so fast, Knightess in Shining Armor. I have a few things I would like to discuss with you."

"We have nothing to discuss unless you let my friends go."

"Ah-h-h, I think we do. If you will remember, when you were a guest in my palace..."

"Guest?"

"I like to think of it that way," the Commander said with a smirk. "But whatever you want to call it, when we had our last visit, I made you a very generous offer...full partnership in the rule of Crystonia. If I recall correctly, you turned me down."

"You recall correctly," said Carling, her hands clenched so tightly her fingernails were digging into the palms of her hands.

"Well, now the circumstances have changed and I am in a more powerful position. But so you will know what a benevolent leader I am, I will let bygones be bygones. I suggest we start anew."

"What is your new proposal?" Carling demanded, suspicious of his intentions.

"It is very simple: my prisoners for your breastplate," he said slowly, his voice low and menacing.

Carling's thoughts whirled around in her head. On the one hand, she had no desire to be the queen of Crystonia. This had all been thrust upon her without her consent. On the other hand, she didn't like the thought of living in a land ruled by such an evil king. If she said *yes*, what would become of Crystonia? If she said *no*, what would become of Tibbals, Tandum, Manti, Tamah, and Higson?

She reached inside her tunic and ran her hands over the lovely breastplate. It felt cold to the touch. *Is that my answer?* She wondered. Before she had time to change her mind, she reached for the clasps on the sides. Her fingers attempted to unlatch them, but they wouldn't move. She tried harder. Still they held fast. She could not get the breastplate off.

"I can't get it off," she said quietly, looking down at the ground in shame.

"What do you mean?" the Commander snarled.

"It won't come off. I tried."

The Commander whirled and let out a roar from deep within that shook the walls. "So it shall be!" he said as he cantered out of the room.

Carling stood frozen in place, listening to the sound of his retreating hooves. Tears began stinging the backs of her eyes, and when they flowed she let them course down her cheeks without wiping them away. She heard a loud bang as the palace doors slammed shut.

Then silence.

CHAPTER 18

The Tommy Knocker
Reappears

CARLING BEGAN PACING, TRYING to come up
with a plan. She thought of recruiting help from the
stallions of the Minsheen herd but realized that would
start a battle and she didn't know how prepared they
were to fight the Heilodius Centaurs. She thought next
of the Fauns. If the Commander was taking his prisoners
to Fort Heilodius, the Fauns had the advantage of being
somewhat familiar with that fortress, having risked their
own lives to rescue her from the dungeon. But she
needed them to protect the village of Duenton, and she
hesitated to take them away from that important task.

Just as she had determined that she needed to follow
the Heilodius Centaurs and their captives alone, a swirl
of wind brushed her face and lifted her hair and tunic.
She turned toward the door. Standing just inside the
room was Shim.

He placed his finger against his large nose as a
crooked smile appeared on his wrinkled face. Then he

winked one of his large blue eyes as he rested his hands on the top of his crooked cane. "It appears you are in quite a pickle, Miss Carling."

"Hello, Shim. I'm surprised to see you."

"Don't be. I have a special talent. I can appear and disappear whenever I want. And now I want to keep track of you."

"Why are you keeping track of me?"

"Isn't it obvious? You have my beloved stone," he said as he tapped his cane on the ground.

Carling's hand went to the breastplate and protectively covered the red Stone of Courage. "Can you help me, then?" she asked, doubting his response would be in the affirmative.

"If I feel like it," Shim answered, raising his bushy eyebrows.

Carling didn't really know how to respond to this odd creature who always seemed to speak in riddles. The Duende were honest and forthright in their communications. "Um...well...do you *feel* like it?"

"As a matter of fact, I do...at the moment."

"Great! A man of your talents could really be helpful."

He tapped his cane again. "You best tell me what the problem is before I change my mind."

Carling recounted the events of the night. "They are taking them to Fort Heilodius," she concluded.

Shim spun around and disappeared before Carling could say anything more. But before she even had a chance to leave the room, Shim was back. "They are in the middle of the Forest of Rumors. They were easy to find; your friend, Tibbals, was making quite a ruckus. It appears she doesn't like being tied up."

Carling frowned and said, "Poor Tibbals." Looking directly into Shim's eyes, she added, "That's the most direct route to Fort Heilodius."

"It appears so. Now what do you want to do?"

Carling dropped to the floor, crossed her legs, and rested her chin in her hands. "I have to think."

"How long is that going to take you?" said Shim. "I don't have all day, you know."

"I can't think with you talking all the time."

"Excuse me. Maybe I should just leave," Shim said, tapping his cane loudly on the floor.

Carling looked up at Shim and frowned. "Do you have any suggestions?"

"Well, I know just what to do," he said, stomping one of his large pointed boots.

"And just what would that be?" Carling asked with some measure of skepticism.

Shim pulled a water flask from his belt. "I'd simply give them some of this," he said, holding up the flask and smiling broadly.

Suddenly, everything became very clear to Carling. "You! You're the one who poisoned the Fauns."

"Well, that seems a bit harsh, don't you think? I just made them a little sick."

"A *little* sick. They all nearly died. If it hadn't been for Contessa figuring out that it was Nightspell, they would have."

"Well, how was I to know they would be so sensitive to it? After all, some races aren't affected by it at all. I've tried it on the Cyclops and they don't blink an eye!"

"Why did you do that in the first place?"

Shim twirled his cane over his head, spun around, and disappeared.

The sun was just rising in the east, sending its warm rays sliding sideways across the room. In the approaching light, Carling heard Shim's voice. "I'm not going to help you if you are mean to me."

Carling felt her stomach tighten with irritation. She slapped her knees with her hands. "Shim, quit playing games. I have a serious problem and I need to know if I can count on your help or not. If not, FINE! Go away and let me think."

In a twinkle, Shim reappeared. "So you want to know why I poisoned the Fauns?"

"That would be helpful, yes."

"I didn't want them to help you."

Carling started, her violet eyes opening wide. "So you knew all along that I was to retrieve your beloved stone?"

"Maybe I did. Maybe I didn't."

"No games, Shim."

"Okay, I knew. But I didn't know exactly when you would be sent by the Wizard to take it from me. I just wanted to delay it as long as possible."

"But the Fauns don't know anything about the Stones of Light."

Shim shrugged as though this information meant nothing to him. "They were helping you. That's all I knew."

Carling took a deep breath and let it out loudly. She could see this discussion was not getting them anywhere. She made a mental note to never trust Shim. "Well, let's put that aside for now," she said. "We have to figure out a way to save my friends from the Commander. What is your idea about using Nightspell?"

"Well, while I haven't tried this on Centaurs before, I have discovered that a more diluted dose acts like a sleeping potion. My idea is to use it on the Centaurs while they camp in the Forest of Rumors tonight."

"How will you get them to drink it?"

Shim's large blue eyes twinkled. "I happen to know the Heilodius Centaurs have a weakness for wine and strong drink."

CHAPTER 19

Brisby

WHILE SHIM HAD THE unique ability to disappear and reappear whenever and wherever he liked, Carling wasn't blessed with such a talent. As soon as Shim disappeared from Manti's chambers, Carling dashed out the palace doors, running as quickly as her not-yet-perfect leg would allow her.

The residents of the city of Minsheen were just waking up and starting their daily activities. Carling paid them no notice as she ran toward the city gates. No one stopped her or questioned why she was in such a hurry. The absence of Manti and Tamah had not been noticed or noised about as yet.

Once in the Forest of Rumors, it was quite easy to follow the route taken by the Commander and his soldiers. Tangled vines were ripped down and thick undergrowth was trampled, making it easy to see where they had gone.

Carling ran for longer than she'd thought she'd be able, but eventually her energy was spent and her leg began to pulsate with pain. She had to stop and rest. She kneeled down on a soft patch of moss to catch her breath.

The little Duende had no idea how far she had run nor how far ahead the Heilodius Centaurs and their captives were. As she rested, she came to the discouraging realization that, despite the fact she had long legs for a Duende, she would never be able to catch up with the Heilodius Centaurs as they cantered through the Forest of Rumors.

Carling took a deep breath of the damp forest air, smelling the moist soil and ripe foliage. Her mouth was dry and she looked around for a source of water. Nothing.

She heard forest creatures moving around her and felt herself shiver. A branch cracked sharply and some crows alighted from their perches overhead, crying out in complaint at being disturbed. Carling wrapped her arms around her body as she turned her head from side to side. She felt very alone.

"Shim?" she called out. "Are you there?"

No answer.

"Wizard, can you see me?"

No response.

A squirrel scolded her from a drooping tree branch, causing her to jump to her feet in alarm. Her heart pounding, she whirled around, then peered into the thick brush, jerking her head from side to side. She was sure something or someone was hiding there watching her.

Turning to the right, Carling saw something that made her heart turn over. A single eye gleamed in the darkness of the underbrush.

She bit her bottom lip and felt the Stone of Courage grow warm against her body. Standing up to her full three-and-a-half-foot height, she said, "I see you there. Present yourself."

The eye blinked, then rose up above the gnarled brush.

When she saw who the eye belonged to, Carling started and stepped back. Standing before her was a Cyclops. But this Cyclops was only about half the size of the Cyclops she had seen in the Echoing Plains when she was traveling to find the Stone of Mercy. And, again, half the size of the Cyclops she had seen battling the Heilodius Centaurs after escaping from the dungeon in the Commander's fortress. Still, he was huge compared to her, and she was so stunned at his sudden appearance that all words escaped her. She stood and stared at him, her eyes wide, her mouth open.

The Cyclops spoke first. "What is a little Duende girl like you doing alone in the Forest of Rumors?"

"I...I...I'm on my way to find my friends."

"Your friends? Where are they?"

"The Heilodius Centaurs are taking them to Fort Heilodius," said Carling. For some inexplicable reason, Carling was starting to feel less threatened by this Cyclops. "Now can I ask about you?" she added.

"What do you want to know about me?"

"Are you all alone in the forest as well?"

The Cyclops' eyelid drooped, half hooding his large eye in the center of his forehead. He nodded slowly.

"Why are *you* here alone?" asked Carling, sensing the creature's sorrow.

The Cyclops stepped over and through the tangled brush. Carling held her ground.

"If you must know, I've run away."

"Run away from whom?" asked Carling.

"From the other Cyclops in my village on the edge of Manyon Canyon."

"Why?"

The Cyclops dropped his horned head and shuffled his hairy feet. "Can't you tell? I don't fit in."

"I still don't understand," said Carling, kindly.

"I'm too short. I'm a RUNT!" he said as a big tear fell to the ground from his eye. "I got tired of being teased all the time. So I ran away."

"You've been belittled?"

The Cyclops jerked his head up. "BELITTLED! There you go. You're teasing me, too! Just like everyone in my village." He moaned and dropped his ugly face in his huge hands.

"Oh, I'm so sorry. I didn't mean it that way...it's just a word that means to be made fun of."

"Yeah, well words can hurt, you know," he said, the sound of his voice muffled by the hair on his hands that were still covering his face.

Carling stepped forward and patted the Cyclops on his round belly, which was as high up as she could reach. "I'm truly, truly sorry. I'll be more careful with the words I choose."

"Thank you. I would appreciate that," he said, sniffing loudly. "Nobody wants me around. They never have. When I was young, no one would ever pick me for any of the games, not for 'Catch the Faun,' or 'Eye Spy,' or even 'Blind Cyclops Bluff.'" He let out another mournful moan.

Carling nodded. "That must have been so hard."

"It was. And now that I'm old, no one wants me in their army. They say I won't be any good at fighting, that I'm too short to see the enemy."

"I see why you are so unhappy. I even think I can understand."

"How could you understand? You're not short, at least not compared to other Duende."

"True. But I'm *tall*. Sometimes I would get teased for being so tall. I can't tell you how many times my schoolmates said, 'How's the weather up there?' I got really tired of hearing that. And no one wanted to dance with me...except Higson."

The mention of Higson's name brought the reality of the situation Carling was facing crashing down upon her. "I...I...have to get going. It was nice meeting you."

Carling turned and started running down the trail created by the Centaurs.

"Wait. Wait for me," said the Cyclops. In three long, loping steps, he caught up with her. Carling kept running; the Cyclops walked. "I want to come with you."

"As you wish."

"Now that we are friends, what do I call you?" he said, slowing down to keep pace with her.

Carling stopped and turned to look at her new companion. "I'm so sorry. That was rude of me. I am Carling."

"And I am Brisby. It is nice to meet you, new friend Carling," the Cyclops said, extending his furry hand. He smiled, black, jagged teeth showing behind thin lips.

Carling smiled back and took his hand. She never imagined that Cyclops would have such wonderful manners. *I have a lot to learn about the other races,* she thought to herself.

Help from a New Friend

"NOW THAT WE'RE FRIENDS," said Brisby, "I think I should help you."

"Help me? How?" said Carling as she got set to start running again. She brushed her auburn curls off her sticky forehead, sucked in as much air as her lungs would hold, and set her eyes on the path ahead.

"I think I should carry you. I can run much faster than you can."

Carling turned and looked up at Brisby. "You'd do that?"

"Sure I would. You're my friend. I have to help you."

"That would be wonderful," said Carling, her muscles already at their limit, her lungs already aching for air, her heart already throbbing with fatigue. And none of this took into account the strain she was putting on her leg.

Brisby scooped Carling up as though she was as light as a breath of wind and set her on his shoulders. "Hold on to my horn," he said.

Carling clasped the single horn that protruded out of the center of the Cyclops' head. Her thin legs hung down his chest and nestled against his fur.

"Where to, madam?"

"Let's follow the trail left by the Centaurs."

"As you say," said Brisby with a chuckle. He held on to her ankles with both hands and started running.

Unlike the smooth rocking gate of the Centaurs when they cantered, Brisby's two-legged strides were choppy. Carling bounced up and down with each long, quick step the Cyclops took. But he was right about one thing: Brisby was much faster and covered far more ground than Carling ever could.

The sun painted the clouds scarlet and purple as it sank below the western horizon. The painted sky was reflected in the mirror-like waters of Lake Mantle.

None of this beauty was noticed by any in the group of tired and irritable travelers on the eastern shores of the lake. The Commander came to a halt. "We'll stop here for tonight."

Grumbles spread through the line of soldiers.

"It's about time."

"Is he trying to kill us?"

"I didn't think I could take another step."

"My hooves are killing me."

Some of the Centaurs just flopped over on their sides and began snoring. Others stepped up to the shore of the lake to get a long and much-needed drink of water.

The Commander walked to the back where Manti, Tamah, Tibbals, Tandum, and Higson stood huddled together, still bound with ropes. Tamah had collapsed to the ground and was rubbing her sore hooves. Tibbals was running her fingers through her long blond hair in an attempt to detangle it. Manti, Tandum, and Higson were standing with their arms crossed tightly across their chests and frowns on their faces.

"Brother, why are you doing this? What do you hope to accomplish?" asked Manti, his eyes filled with sadness as he questioned his brother.

"What do I hope to accomplish? I think you know the answer to that."

"I understand your ultimate goal is to rule Crystonia. But what do we have to do with any of that? Why are you taking me and my family?"

"You are nothing more than bait, dear brother. My desire is to get to our little Carling through you."

"And what then? What will you do with us?"

The Commander shrugged. "I don't know. I guess that depends upon you. If you are willing to sign a treaty with me saying you will either support my rule or, at the very least, stay out of my way and not interfere, maybe I'll let you go. Maybe."

"But what of Carling?" Higson nearly shouted, his fists clenched at his sides. "What are you planning to do with her?"

The Commander looked down at Higson and narrowed his eyes. "That will depend entirely upon her. I have already made her a very generous offer on two different occasions."

"And she turned you down," said Higson.

"Yes. Very shortsighted of her."

"So now what?" inquired Tibbals.

"Because I want to show what a magnanimous leader I am, I am willing to make her yet another offer. But mind you, my patience is running thin. She slipped through my hooves once. I don't intend to let that happen again. Either she agrees to work with me, or she will pay the price."

Even with his large single eye, Brisby found that the moonless night made it difficult to see the trail of smashed undergrowth and maneuver through the Forest of Rumors. But the Cyclops kept going as quickly as he could run.

Carling and Brisby approached the Centaur's camp well after the sun fell below the western horizon. They could hear the Centaurs talking and laughing even before they saw them. The first sign of the Centaur camp was the dancing shadows cast by their campfire. Brisby stopped and ducked behind a large tree with low branches. "I see them up ahead," he whispered.

"So do I," said Carling.

Just then, a whirl of wind caught the branches beside them, rattling the leaves.

Shim appeared. "Well, it's about time you caught up with me," he said.

"Shim, I can't just pop in and out like you can. If Brisby hadn't decided to help me, I'd still be a very long way away."

"So, you have a new friend. How sweet. Puny, isn't he?"

Brisby growled. "I'm big enough to take care of the likes of you," he sneered.

"Shim, Brisby does not like to be told he's small."

"Oh, please pardon me, won't you? I have a bad habit of stating the obvious," said Shim, only adding to Brisby's angst.

Carling swung one leg over Brisby's shoulder and slid to the ground. "Arguing is not going to get us anywhere," she said, glaring at Shim. "Nor is it helpful to insult one another."

Shim crossed his arms over his chest, let out a humph, and turned his back on them.

Carling ignored this. "Shim, I am looking to you for the best ideas of what to do next. You mentioned a sleeping potion..."

Shim spun around, a broad smile spread across his face. Lifting one finger in the air, he said, "Perhaps our little friend here can be useful after all."

"Shim...," said Carling, shaking her finger.

"Oh, yes. Sorry. Well, as I was saying, Nightspell doesn't affect Cyclops." Shim stopped and turned to face Brisby. "You *are* a real Cyclops, aren't you?"

Brisby rose up to his full height and firmly planted his fists on his hips. "Of course I am."

"Good. That's very good. My idea is to send Bristles here..."

"Brisby," corrected Carling.

With a wave of his hand, Shim said, "Whatever. Let's send *Brisby* here into the camp with the flask of diluted Nightspell. He can drink some of it right in front of them, then offer each of them a swig. If I know the Heilodius Centaurs, they won't be able to resist."

"But...but...what if they try to hurt me?" stammered Brisby.

"Play it by ear. Make sure they know you are alone, and they shouldn't be threatened by you."

"What if they think I'm just a spy?"
"Get them drinking before they think that far."
And so it was decided.

CHAPTER 21

Sleep Tight Centaurs

THE THREE COMPANIONS, THEY could not yet be described as friends, crept up closer to the campsite. They crouched behind a row of prickly bushes, and surveyed the scene before them. The Heilodius Centaurs were settled in around the campfire, too tired to do much more than talk and tell a few Centaur Jokes.

"Why did the Centaur filly start singing at the party?"

"I don't know. Why?"

"Because she wanted to be the Centaur of attention!"

All of the Centaurs thought this was terribly funny.

Shim just rolled his eyes. "Sometimes I think Centaurs are given way too much credit for being intelligent," he whispered.

Off to one side, well away from the fire, Manti, Tamah, Tibbals, Tandum, and Higson were crowded together and tied up with ropes. "Brisby," whispered Carling, her hand and face against his tiny ear. "See those Centaurs over there by that fallen tree?" she said, motioning with her other hand toward where Tibbals and her family were resting.

Brisby nodded.

"Make sure you don't give them any of the Nightspell. That's who we're trying to rescue."

"Got it," he said. "What about the Duende that's with them? Do we want him?"

"Yes. That's my best friend."

"I thought *I* was your best friend."

Carling patted him on his hairy shoulder. "You're getting there." She gave him her warmest smile.

This seemed to satisfy the Cyclops, who smiled back.

"Let me interrupt this love fest," said Shim. He stretched his hand toward the Cyclops, a flask dangling from his wrist by a shiny red cord. "Here's the sleeping potion. It won't affect you. You just need to get the Heilodius Centaurs to drink it. Got it?"

"Got it," said Brisby. He reached out his clawed hand and took the flask. Opening the cap, he sniffed. "Yum. This smells good."

"Don't waste it. That's all I have at the moment. Just let them each take a little sip. They'll want more but don't let them have it."

Brisby stepped around the gnarled tree and into the light of the campfire. "So what's going on here?" he asked the Centaurs.

All of the Centaurs turned to look at the intruder. The Commander leaped up onto all four hooves. "What do you think you're doing here?"

Brisby took a swig from the flask and hiccupped. "I think I've lost my way." *Hic.* "Perhaps you can direct me toward Manyon Canyon." *Hic.*

"Manyon Canyon? You're a long way from there," said the Commander, his eyes narrowed with suspicion. "Where is the rest of your tribe?"

Hic. "That's the problem." *Hic.* "I haven't seen them for days. I've been wandering around this frightening forest looking for them. Good thing I have my friend here to keep me happy," he said, patting the flask and hiccupping loudly a few more times.

Another Centaur stood and stepped forward. "Say, what's in the flask anyway?"

Brisby took another swig. "It's the best darn elixir ever invented. It's a secret recipe known only to Cyclops."

The Centaur licked his lips. "Can I give it a try? Just a little taste, mind you."

"We-e-e-ll. I don't know. I don't have that much left."

"Just a sip," urged the Centaur again.

"I guess it can't hurt," Brisby said, feigning reluctance. Scrunching up his black lips, he extended the flask. The Centaur grabbed it. "Just a sip," Brisby reminded him.

From the edge of the clearing, Carling and Shim watched with excitement as the Centaur held the flask above his mouth and squeezed a stream of the Nightspell into his mouth. Carling turned and grinned at Shim. The Tommy Knocker just smirked.

Brisby snatched the flask away from the Centaur. "That's enough. I told you just a sip."

The Centaur smacked his lips and rolled his eyes. "Ahhhh. I've never tasted anything so good."

"I told you," said Brisby, cradling his flask like a baby.

This caught the attention of all of the Centaurs.

"Hey, can I try it?"

"Share it with the rest of us!"

"I'm dying to try it, too!"

The Centaurs shoved each other as they struggled to get close to Brisby.

"Ouch, you're stepping on my hoof!"

"Hey, he pulled my tail!"

The Commander raised his hand and stomped one front hoof. "Settle down. Settle down. You can try it as soon as I do." He turned to Brisby and extended his open palm. His eyes made it clear that it was a demand, not a request.

Brisby suppressed a smile as he handed the flask to the Commander.

CHAPTER 22

Flight Through the Forest

FROM THEIR HIDING PLACE behind the prickly brush, Carling and Shim watched as, one by one, the Centaurs dropped to their knees and hocks and rolled onto their sides. Soon, they were all fast asleep and snoring loudly.

"I gotta give it to the little beast...he's good," whispered Shim.

Carling smiled and nodded.

Brisby strutted around the campfire, clearly proud of himself, and motioned for Carling to join him.

Carling dashed into the clearing.

"Carling!" shouted Higson.

"Sh-h-h-h," cautioned the others.

Carling ran up to the captives and began untying the ropes. Brisby joined her.

"Strange company you keep," Tibbals whispered through the side of her mouth as Carling untied her. Carling only chuckled.

When all of the captives were untied, Manti took command. "Tamah and Tibbals, how are you feeling? Can you keep going?"

Tamah checked each of her hooves. "I'm a bit hoof-sore, but I'll be fine."

Tibbals stretched her arms out to the side. "With those nasty ropes finally off me, I feel like I could canter all night."

"Good, because I'm afraid we're going to have to," said Manti. He turned and led the group, single file, past the sleeping Heilodius Centaurs. They tiptoed on the front of their hooves so as not to awaken any of their captors. When he came to the Commander, Manti stopped. Shaking his head, he whispered, "Goodbye, dear brother. I'm deeply sorry it has come to this."

Tamah stepped up beside her stallion and placed her hands on either side of his face. She gently kissed him. "Let's go," she said quietly.

Tandum also stepped up. "If only I had my sword...," he said as he glared down at the Commander.

Tibbals pulled him away. "Let's go," she said.

As they left the clearing and started cantering through the Forest of Rumors, Carling looked for Shim. She turned her head from side to side but saw no sign of him. She felt an ache of sadness inside, sadness that she hadn't had a chance to thank him for his help. She sighed and pursed her lips. Perhaps he would show up again when he was least expected. Slowly, she turned back to face the way they were going.

They cantered until they could canter no more. The going was difficult, even for four-legged creatures. The path on which they had come was difficult to see in the darkness, and the Centaurs found themselves stumbling frequently on concealed rocks and fallen branches. Tree branches reached out to grab them like the fingers of skeletons. The night creatures taunted them.

Brisby, on the other hand, actually managed well compared to the others. He took the lead and kept them on the trail. Brisby's only issue was that his large eye kept attracting little insects. Gnats and mosquitoes seemed to be attracted to the glowing orb. He had to keep stopping to wipe a bug from his eye with his long, pointed tongue. It was quite unpleasant to watch.

At a stream crossing, they stopped for a much-needed rest.

"How is everyone doing?" asked Manti.

"Can we sleep for a while?" Tibbals said with a moan.

"I'm afraid not, my dear," he answered with a sympathetic smile. "We don't know how long the Heilodius will sleep. They could, even now, be on our tails."

Tibbals sighed. "You're right, of course. Mount up, Carling," the filly said.

Through the rest of the night, they continued on, moving in silence, too tired to speak. By first light, they lifted their eyes and gazed at the sparkling white towers of Minsheen.

"I will be leaving you, now," said Brisby.

"Why?" said Carling, shocked and disappointed. "Don't you want to stay with us?"

"No. I don't belong in that city. I would stand out like a wart on your cute little nose!"

Carling rubbed her nose without thinking about it.

Manti stepped over to Brisby. "I understand if you would feel uncomfortable in the city of Minsheen. After all, our races have not been on the best of terms. But we owe our lives to you. You would be under our protection."

Brisby smiled. "Thank you, great Centaur leader. But I think I will gather the courage to return to my people." He looked down at Carling. "I will be your protector whenever you need me. We will always be best friends."

"Yes," said Carling. "Best friends."

Brisby started to walk in the direction of Manyon Canyon. He stopped suddenly. "By the way, where did that funny little man go that was with us in the forest? The one who gave me the flask of Nightspell."

"Oh, that's Shim." Carling shook her head and smiled. "I never know when he will show up or when he will leave."

Carling didn't leave her room for a full day and night, so tired was she. Sleeping was interrupted only by the throbbing in her leg.

The following day, Chamay came to her room to check on her. She pushed open the door and entered the room, balancing a breakfast tray on her broad back. "Are you ever going to wake up, little queen?"

Carling opened one eye. "Do I have to?"

Chamay chuckled. "Well, only of you want some of this delicious breakfast the cooks have made for you."

Carling pushed back the warm covers, stretched her arms over her head, and sat up. "Yum-m-m-m," she said with a smile. "That smells wonderful."

Chamay fluffed up and propped some pillows behind Carling. Then she checked the Duende's leg. Carling flinched as her healer poked at her. Chamay stood upright and shook her head, a frown on her face.

"You've not been a good patient, Miss Carling. I'm going to have to put this leg back in my special wrap."

Chamay disappeared out the door, reappearing a short time later with the special bands she'd used to wrap Carling's leg. The healer went to work spreading a thick, foul-smelling salve over the leg and wrapping it tightly with the bands. Carling could immediately feel heat penetrating to the bone. Her leg began to tingle, almost to the point of pain.

When she was done, Chamay stood. Her hands placed firmly on her hips, she said, "Now I mean it when I say I want you to stay off this leg." The healer shook her head again. "Tsk, tsk. And I *really* mean it!" she said, then headed toward the door.

"Chamay," called Carling.

Chamay stopped and turned around. She tilted her head and swished her tail, waiting for Carling to continue speaking.

"How are Tibbals, Tandum, and Higson?"

"I haven't seen them. I don't believe any of them have emerged from their rooms since all of you returned from your nighttime adventures." She paused and twisted her mouth to one side. "Perhaps someday you will tell me why the six of you were gallivanting around in the Forest of Rumors through all hours of the night."

CHAPTER 23

An Epistle

MANTI WAS PACING IN the Council Chambers, his face painted with sadness, his heart heavy with sorrow. A knock on the door brought him out of his reverie.

"Come in."

One of his assistants opened the door and stepped into the room. In his hand, he held a scroll. This he placed on one of the desks. "This just came for you, sir. A Heilodius Centaur is, even now, in the atrium, awaiting your response."

Manti eyed the scroll, curious. "Thank you."

His assistant bowed and backed out of the room, closing the doors behind him.

Manti unrolled the scroll, smoothed it out over the table, and started reading.

Manti, most noble lead stallion of the Minsheen herd.

Behold, I write this epistle unto you and do give unto you exceeding great praise because of your firmness in maintaining that which ye suppose to be the right course of action.

And it seemeth a pity unto me, most noble brother, that ye should be so naïve as to cling to the foolish traditions of our fathers and put your trust and faith in the wearer of a trivial Silver Breastplate to be the chosen ruler of our land.

Do ye suppose that ye can stand against so many brave Centaurs who are at my command, who do now at this time stand at arms and do await with great anxiety for a word from me to go down upon your city and destroy you and your Centaurs of the Minsheen herd? If they should come down against you, they would visit you with utter destruction.

Therefore, I have written this epistle, sealing it with mine own hand, feeling for your welfare and the welfare of your family, because of your firmness in that which I realize ye believe to be right.

Therefore, I write unto you, desiring that ye would meet with me, face to face, and in a secret meeting place of your choosing that we might come to a truce and call a halt to the conflict between us as brothers.

If ye will not do this, I swear unto you with an oath that on the morrow I will command that my armies shall come down against you and your herd, and they shall not stay their hand until ye shall become extinct.

I await your immediate response for, behold, I am the Commander, the ruler of the Heilodius herd.

Manti looked up from the scroll. Perspiration was rolling down his face and chest. His hands were trembling. Never had he imagined his own brother would threaten to start a civil war among the Centaurs.

He stepped up to one of the tall windows that lined the side of the room. From this vantage point, he could just see Mount Heilodius peeking around from behind

Mount Dashmore. He stood in silent contemplation for several minutes.

Finally, the kind and gentle Centaur sighed and turned back around, stepping over to his desk. From the center drawer of the desk, he removed a small piece of parchment, a quill pen, and a bottle of ink. Putting pen to paper, he began writing his response.

Dear Brother, the Commander of the Heilodius herd.

It is with heavy heart that I received and read your epistle. As you recorded, I am, indeed, firm and steadfast in my faith in the traditions of our fathers. I have awaited, with some degree of impatience, for the arrival of the wearer of the Silver Breastplate, the rightful heir to the throne of Crystonia.

While I understand that you do not hold to the same beliefs, I am shocked and disheartened that you are willing to spill the blood of your brothers and sisters in order to secure your own vain ambitions.

Therefore, in order to do all I can to prevent such a tragic calamity, I will acquiesce to your request for a secret meeting, though I doubt anything can be resolved.

Let us meet at the hollow tree just outside the city walls where we once frolicked as young colts. I shall await your arrival as the sun sets.

Your brother, Manti, lead stallion of the Minsheen herd.

Manti rolled up the parchment and summoned his aide, instructing him to deliver it to the Commander's servant in the atrium. Then he returned to his quarters to spend the afternoon in quiet contemplation.

Just as the sun approached the horizon, Manti, concealed beneath a hooded cloak, snuck silently out a small door on the side of the city wall. He glanced both ways, then cantered to his childhood playground in front of an old hollow tree.

The Commander was waiting for him. "Thank you for coming, dear brother," the large, muscled Centaur said. His black and silver uniform caught the last of the sun's rays and made him look even more foreboding than he already was.

Manti nodded briefly. "You gave me little choice, Polson."

The Commander winced at the sound of his given name. "I prefer to be called 'Commander.'"

"Forgive me. Old habits are hard to break," Manti said. "Shall we get to the business at hand?"

The Commander swished his tail, a sign of his impatience. "We shall. Let me state my position. As I stated in your chambers, I do not intend to be ruled by a little Duende girl, breastplate or no breastplate. I will give you one last chance to join me, my brother."

Manti stared into the coal black eyes of this Centaur he had once loved so dearly. This is the Centaur he had grown up with and spent his colthood with. They had run and bucked in the meadows. They had played hide-and-seek in the forest. They had teased the young fillies of the herd. But now all of that was gone, never to return.

"No, Polson. I cannot do that."

A sneer spread across the Commander's face. His eyes narrowed until they were nothing but slits the width of twine. "So be it!" he shouted.

Suddenly, four Heilodius Centaurs burst forth from behind some nearby trees, surrounding them. Swords held high, they galloped toward Manti. Their weapons flashed in the dim light of dusk. When they were done with their dastardly deed, Manti lay in his own blood, his lifeless eyes staring up at the Commander.

CHAPTER 24

Facing the Commander

CARLING HAD CHOSEN THIS same evening to stretch her legs and get some fresh air. She felt cooped up, having been in her room for several days so her leg could heal. She put on her Silver Breastplate, covered it with a cloak, and headed out of her room. A sudden strange thought entered her head and she returned for her sword, concealing it in the folds of her cape.

The young Duende went out the palace doors. She paused long enough to take a deep breath of the cool evening air. She noticed the scent of the roses that climbed the trellises around the city parks. She loved the feel of the gentle breeze as it kissed her skin. With a smile on her face, she started walking. The sun had just set but the sky was still aglow with streaks of gold and magenta. She couldn't take her eyes off the beautiful scene.

As she came upon Centaurs in the city, she acknowledged them with a smile and a nod but didn't stop to talk. Rather, with a pronounced limp, she continued walking. She avoided the large city square and the ornate front gates, not wanting to talk to anyone. She desired only to be alone with her thoughts.

Carling turned up a narrow street she had never walked up before. It was lined with well-maintained Centaur stables. She glanced in the occasional window and noticed the Centaur families gathering for their evening meal. A pang of sorrow filled her as she recalled the many family dinners she'd had with her mother and father. She missed that. She missed them. She suddenly felt very alone. She sighed and bit her lower lip as she continued on.

Carling walked haltingly to the end of the street and around a corner where the little road ended abruptly at the city wall. Set into the wall was a door, small by Centaur standards but large for Carling. The door stood slightly ajar. Carling hobbled up to the door, wrapped her fingers around the edge, and pulled the door open. It creaked loudly on its hinges as it swung inward.

A tingle of excitement filled her as she stepped through the doorway, as though she was doing something she shouldn't. She laughed out loud at her silliness and nearly skipped, as best she could, toward the trees that covered the sides of Mount Dashmore.

Just as she entered the forest, she heard voices. She stopped and listened. Carling immediately recognized the voices as belonging to Manti and the Commander.

"So be it," she heard the Commander roar.

Carling's heart seemed to stop. She clasped a low branch to keep herself upright. With teeth clenched, she forced her legs to move, stumbling through the forest toward the sound of shouts and cries. The brave, young girl stepped into the clearing just in time to see Manti take his final blow and fall to the ground, where he lay still, staring up at his brother.

"No-o-o-o-o," Carling cried.

The Commander whirled around toward her and charged, swinging his sword in a circle above his head.

Carling couldn't move very fast with her injured leg nearly hobbling her. However, she was quick enough to duck and roll beneath a bent-over tree. The Commander's sword crashed down, splintering the tree in two. Carling crawled on her hands and knees deeper into the shelter of the branches as the Commander slashed away, trying to find her. He was soon joined by the other Heilodius Centaurs.

It was getting dark, and the Centaurs were having trouble seeing into the shadows that were concealing Carling. She scurried on her hands and knees as quickly as she could, away from where the Commander was still chopping at the tree, growling and cursing as he did so. She could see his hooves stomping the ground and the broken branches. The Commander shouted orders to his soldiers, directing them where to look.

Carling paused to catch her breath and pull her sword from the folds of her cloak. She peeked through the branches and vines, squinting to get a better look. She watched with bated breath as the Commander's front legs left the ground and came down among the branches just in front of her. She figured she would have just one chance to attack the Commander under the cover of darkness. The element of surprise could be used to her advantage.

The young Duende felt the red Stone of Courage grow hot against her skin. She clenched her jaw, clasped her sword with both hands, and lunged forward.

The Commander let out a mighty howl as Carling's sword pierced his side.

Still clutching her sword, which was now stained with the Commander's blood, Carling fell backward and rolled back into the underbrush. The four Centaurs who'd attacked Manti descended on the brush, thrashing and tearing at the vines and branches, searching for Carling.

"Leave her," said the Commander as he gasped in pain. "I am wounded. We must return to the Fort." He and his four soldiers all turned and cantered away into the dark of night.

CHAPTER 25

Wrongly Accused

CARLING CROUCHED BENEATH THE brush until silence returned to the forest. Once it did, she crawled out into the clearing, stood up, and limped over to where Manti lay on the ground, his blood staining the grass around him. Pain filled her heart and, with a moan, she dropped to her knees beside him.

"Manti, oh Manti," she cried. Tears streamed down her cheeks as she started sobbing.

Just as she attempted to get a hold of herself by taking a deep breath, she realized she wasn't alone. She jumped up and whirled around. Shim was standing behind her, only a few feet away, clearly visible in the darkness.

"Shim," she exclaimed. "You frightened me."

"I came to warn you to leave immediately. The Centaurs are searching for Manti. It will not look good for you to be found here."

"Why not? I have nothing to hide. I will tell them what happened."

"Do as you wish. But remember that I tried to warn you," Shim said. With a cock of his head and a twitch of his big nose, he twirled his cane above his head. Instantly, the Tommy Knocker disappeared.

Just as he did so, two large Centaurs from the Minsheen herd crashed into the clearing, lanterns held high above their heads. Carling turned to face them, still clutching her bloody sword.

"Oh, thank goodness you have come," she started to say.

"What is going on here?" said one, interrupting her as he and his companion ran up to Manti's lifeless body.

Realizing immediately that their leader was dead, they turned on Carling. "What have you done?" they both cried, their voices reflecting their shock and anger.

"Me? I have done nothing. I came upon him just as the Commander and his soldiers were attacking him."

"We do not see the Commander, nor any soldiers," snarled one of the Centaurs. "We see only you standing over Manti with a blood-stained sword."

Carling released her grip on the sword, letting it fall to the ground. "You misunderstand. My sword bears the blood of the Commander."

They scoffed at this. "We do not see the Commander. Nor do we believe you would be able to battle with the likes of *him*," said one. He grabbed hold of her arm, squeezing tightly. "I think you better come with me," he said.

The other bent down and picked up the Duende's sword. "Let's get back," he said. "We'll send others to bring Manti to the city."

Carling wasn't taken back to her lovely, comfortable room. Instead, she was picked up and dropped into a closet beneath a staircase. With a click, the door was locked, and there she remained for the rest of the night.

The closet was dark and silence filled the tiny space, which smelled of musty rags and mold. Carling sat on the rough, wooden floor and leaned against the back wall, making herself as comfortable as possible. She pulled her knees up to her chin, breathed in the stale air, and tried to calm her pounding heart.

How did I get myself into this mess? she thought. *And how am I going to get out of it? What could I have done? What should I have done?* Her thoughts bounced from confusion to regret to sorrow. When she thought of Manti lying dead in the forest, she couldn't help but cry. And when she thought of Tibbals, Tandum, and Tamah, she cried even harder.

Her thoughts were interrupted by a tapping sound coming from inside the closet. She looked around but could see nothing in the darkness.

The tapping stopped and Carling heard a gravelly voice. "Well, it seems you've made quite a mess of things. Such a pity. Such a pity."

"Oh, it's you, Shim," Carling said as the creature appeared, surprised at how happy she was that he was suddenly with her. *I guess anything beats being alone in a smelly closet,* she said to herself.

"I tried to warn you to get away from there," Shim said, wagging a finger at Carling. "But did you listen to me? No!"

"I couldn't just leave Manti alone."

"He was dead, wasn't he? What good could you do at that point?"

"Do you have any feelings in that heart of yours?" Carling asked, disgusted.

"Not many. Why should I? Feeling just gets you in trouble. The way I see it, using my brain is a better idea than using my heart."

"I think that's a sad way to live," said Carling, lowering her chin onto her knees.

"Well, it doesn't look like you're really happy right now."

"No. I'm not."

"Well, let me repeat. I tried to warn you!" With that, a twinkle of light appeared in the dark closet and Shim disappeared.

At some point in the night, Carling dozed off out of pure exhaustion, but for how long she could not tell. The clicking of Centaur hooves outside the door awakened her with a start.

"You put her in here?" It was Tibbals.

Carling jumped up. "Tibbals. Tibbals, is that you?"

She heard a key turn in the lock. The door opened, letting in a beam of light that stung Carling's eyes. She squinted as she looked up into Tibbals's face. She knew, immediately, that Tibbals had been informed of her father's fate. Her eyes were puffy and swollen from crying. The two guards who had put Carling in the closet during the night stood stoically behind her.

Carling ran forward, threw her arms around her friend's chest, and cried.

Tibbals did not return the hug, but she did stroke Carling's auburn curls. For quite a while the Centaur filly said nothing. Then Carling heard her sniffling. "Tell me what happened, Carling," Tibbals said.

Carling brushed the tears from her eyes and cheeks, stepped back, and looked directly into her friend's eyes. What she saw frightened her. She had assumed Tibbals would believe her...never doubt her. Yet doubt was what she saw in those swollen eyes.

"Tibbals, I didn't do it. You must believe me."

"The guards found you, with your sword in your hand, standing over my father. Your sword is covered in blood. They showed it to me."

"That isn't your father's blood. That is the Commander's blood."

"The guards only saw you...just you."

"I know. The Commander and four of his soldiers left before the guards arrived."

"And you fought the Commander and his four soldiers alone?" Tibbals said, her voice thick with skepticism.

"I know it sounds hard to believe..."

"Yes. It does."

"You, of all Centaurs, must believe me. You know me. Do you *really* believe I would kill your father?"

Tibbals lowered her head and covered her face with her hands. She started sobbing. "You're right, little Carling. I don't believe you would do such a horrible thing. I'm so sorry I doubted you, my dear, dear friend." The filly bent down and hugged Carling.

Enveloped in Tibbals's arms, Carling felt relief flow through her. She didn't know what she would have done if Tibbals hadn't believed her. Now her thoughts went to Tandum and Higson. Did they know about Manti? Would they doubt her, too?

CHAPTER 26

The Trial

TIBBALS INSISTED THAT THE guards take Carling to her own room but reluctantly acquiesced to their demands that a guard be placed by the suspect's door at all times.

Tibbals spent the day with her mother. Together they mourned the loss of Manti.

Tandum and Higson came to Carling's room when the sun was at its zenith.

"Tell me what happened, Carling," said Tandum, his voice cracking with emotion.

Carling could see the pain in his eyes. She gently recounted her story of going for a walk and hearing the Commander's shout followed by more shouting. She rehearsed her own efforts at survival upon being attacked, concluding with her success in stabbing the Commander in the side of his chest.

Tandum and Higson listened without interruption. When she finished, Higson stepped over to her and took her hands in his. "You could have been killed. It's obvious the Heilodius Centaurs, and the Commander in particular, will stop at nothing to gain the throne. Carling, you simply can't go walking around in the forest alone anymore. Will you promise me you won't do that again?"

Higson's genuine concern touched her heart, and the gratitude she felt for her loyal friend was beyond what words could express. As a result, all Carling could manage was to bite her lip and nod.

Grateful that both Higson and Tandum seemed to believe her account of what had happened, Carling spent some time speaking with them both, trying to reason out the Commander's motives and anticipate his next move. At the same time, she and Higson offered comfort to Tandum on the loss of his father.

Late in the afternoon, two guards opened the door to Carling's room. "You are summoned to the council chambers," one of them said to Carling in a gruff voice. "Prince," the same Centaur said much more politely to Tandum, "we have been instructed to ask you to join your mother and sister in the council chambers so you can serve as royal witnesses."

Carling glanced at Tandum, who lowered his gaze and nodded, then left the room. Then she stood to face the guard who had spoken. "I'm ready," she said.

With Higson by her side, she walked through the hallway and down the wide staircase in silence. Her heart seemed to be beating in rhythm with the clip-clop sound of the Centaurs' hooves. When they reached the council chambers, the doors were ajar, not by way of welcome but rather by way of directive. She took a deep breath and stepped into the room.

Several Centaurs from the Minsheen herd, most of whose names she didn't know but all of whom she had seen before, were seated behind tables. No one smiled at her arrival. They only stared at her, their eyes narrowed.

Carling glanced toward Tibbals, Tandum, and Tamah, who sat over to one side. Concern for them threatened to overwhelm Carling. Feeling the sting of tears behind her eyes, she simply nodded in their direction, grateful when Tibbals gave her a tiny wave.

The little Duende then looked to the other side of the room and noticed Adivino, the herd's historian, sitting behind a desk, the top of a quill pen wiggling as he wrote. She could hear his pen scratching across a piece of parchment. He didn't look up at her.

Carling summoned all the courage provided by the red stone. She set her jaw and approached the tables. "You have called me to appear before you to talk about Manti's murder."

"Yes. There are very serious charges leveled against you," said one, the apparent leader and a Centaur whose name Carling knew to be Zarius.

"I realize that. But they are not true. I did not kill Manti. I would never have killed him. I loved and respected him."

"The evidence seems to contradict that," said Zarius with a stern frown.

"I realize what the guards saw looks bad for me. But they and you have jumped to the wrong conclusion."

"Explain. Tell us what you were doing there."

"I had simply gone for a walk..."

Scoffs and snorts were heard throughout the room.

"No one saw you leave through the city square or the city gates," Zarius said with a sneer. "Why were you being so secretive if you had nothing to hide and were simply going for a walk?"

"It is true that I didn't leave the city through the main gates. I had much on my mind and wanted to be alone."

"Yes, it seems you did," said another Centaur.

Carling glanced over at him before continuing.

"I didn't intend to go to the forest initially. It was only after I stumbled upon a little door in the wall that was ajar that my curiosity got the better of me. I went through the door and into the forest."

"Continue," said Zarius.

"When I was out walking I heard shouts and cries. I ran toward the sounds as fast as I could with my injured leg. When I arrived at the clearing by a big hollow tree, I saw Manti on the ground with four Heilodius Centaurs standing over him. The Commander was standing to one side."

"And how did you get the blood on your sword?" said one of the Centaurs whose name Carling didn't know.

"When I screamed, the Commander charged me. I hid under the brush and tree branches until I had a chance to attack. My sword pierced his side."

"And the other Heilodius soldiers just let you do that?" said another judge with unconcealed incredulity.

"They couldn't find me. It was dark by this time and I had hidden under the tree branches again. They didn't get to search long, however. The Commander insisted that they return to their fort. I think his injury was serious."

"Tell me this," said Zarius. "If you were just out for an evening stroll to get some fresh air, as you say, why did you bring a sword along? To use as a walking stick?"

This brought chuckles from the other judges.

Carling felt the heat of embarrassment and frustration rise to redden her face. "I honestly don't know why I brought it. Just as I was leaving my room, something told me to go back to get it."

For several moments, the judges were silent. Zarius broke the silence. Looking back and forth at the panel, he said, "Let us converse."

The judges stood and left the room through a side door.

Tibbals and Higson dashed up to Carling. "Oh, you poor, poor thing," sobbed Tibbals. "That must have been so horrible for you. I'll bet you were frightened out of your wits."

For the first time, Carling realized she had not been frightened at all. Her hand went to the red Stone of Courage. She was just learning to appreciate how powerful these stones really were.

CHAPTER 27

The Verdict

IT DIDN'T TAKE THE judges long to make their decision, and soon they returned to the room and took their seats. As everyone went back to their places, Carling stood as tall as she was able and looked directly at Zarius.

"We have discussed your testimony and find it too extraordinary to be believed," Zarius said gruffly. "We, therefore, find you guilty of the murder of our beloved lead stallion, Manti."

A gasp went up from the few audience members. Carling didn't move, didn't breathe, didn't even blink an eye. She didn't know what to say or do.

Zarius continued coldly. "Guards, take the prisoner to a cell. She will stay there for the rest of her life."

"No!" shouted Tibbals. "She didn't do it. She's telling the truth. You have to believe her."

Glaring at Tibbals, Zarius bellowed, "Silence in the council chambers or you will be removed!"

Tibbals pursed her lips, pressed her fists against her waist, and glared at Zarius. Tamah reached for her filly, wrapped her arms around her, and stroked her hair.

Just as the guards took hold of Carling, a disturbance erupted in the back of the room. Carling turned and tossed her auburn curls out of her eyes with a flick of her head. What she saw caused her to suck in a quick breath. Pushing their way past the guards and into the room were two Heilodius Centaurs named Bale and Dalt.

Both Centaurs owed their life to Carling. Carling had kept Bale from burning to death in the hunting cabin in the Forest of Rumors. She and Tibbals had saved Dalt from drowning in Lake Mantle. Now, the two of them were forcing their way into the room and trotting up to the front.

"What is the meaning of this?" Zarius demanded, eyeing the two Heilodius Centaurs suspiciously.

"We have come to prevent a grave injustice," said Dalt.

"By this you mean...?" said Zarius, his eyes narrowing.

"I mean you are wrongfully accusing Carling of a crime. She did not kill Manti as you believe. But she may have killed the Commander. He is, even now, on his deathbed and not expected to live."

Zarius cocked his head to one side and eyed the Centaurs with a look of disdain. "Tell us what you know and why you maintain the young Duende is innocent."

"Dalt and I were on guard duty at the gates of Fort Heilodius last night," said Bale. "Sometime during the third watch, the Commander and four of his soldiers came into the fort. The Commander was bleeding badly from a serious wound in his chest."

"After the Commander was assisted to his quarters," added Dalt, "we questioned the four soldiers who had come in with him."

"They told us they had killed Manti but that a little Duende girl had surprised them and attacked the Commander," said Bale.

"We knew right away the only one courageous enough to stand up to the Commander was Carling," said Dalt as he looked down at Carling and smiled.

Every Centaur in the room started talking at once. "Silence! Silence!" shouted Zarius over the din.

When order was restored, Zarius looked down at Carling as she stood silently between the two guards, who were still clutching her arms. "It appears we owe you an apology."

Carling shook her head. "You did what you needed to do. I would probably have done the same, were I in your hooves." She paused and looked from side to side at the guards. "Um-m-m," she said, glancing at Zarius, "can these two release me now?"

CHAPTER 28

Manti's Funeral

AFTER THANKING BALE AND Dalt for their testimony on her behalf, Carling asked her two friends, "What will you do now?"

"We will return to Fort Heilodius," said Bale.

Tibbals and Higson joined the group. "Why don't you stay here?" Tibbals asked. "Surely you don't support the Commander anymore. We would shelter you in the city of Minsheen."

"That is a very kind offer, young filly," said Dalt. "But our absence will be noticed, and we don't want to bring any trouble to your herd."

"In addition," Bale added. "We can keep our eyes and ears open in Fort Heilodius and hoof it right down here to inform Carling if anything arises that she should know about."

After saying their farewells, the two Heilodius Centaurs galloped out of the council chambers to return to their home.

Carling hugged Tibbals and Higson and returned to her room sans guards. It was a good feeling. However, she had a restless night even though she was extremely tired. She kept reliving the night in the clearing, and with each dream the awful scene became more vivid and horrible. The Heilodius Centaurs became increasingly large and loud. Their eyes pierced her with evil. Blood painted the entire forest. She finally forced herself to stay awake as an escape from such terrifying dreams.

She was sitting by her window when the sun first made its appearance and was surprised to hear a soft knock on her door. "Come in," she said.

The door opened slightly and Tibbals peeked into the room. "Are you awake?"

"I am. I didn't sleep very well."

Tibbals stepped into the room and shut the door behind her. "I can understand that. Neither did I." Tibbals sat on Carling's bed and Carling turned to face her, waiting to hear the purpose of her friend's visit.

Tibbals let her shoulders droop and lowered her chin to her chest, letting her long, blond hair fall over her face. The young Duende noticed how ungroomed her friend was, not characteristic of the filly who usually valued her appearance a great deal. Carling's heart swelled with love and empathy. Tibbals was suffering, and Carling wished she could lift the pain that she knew all too well as a result of the loss of her own parents. She stood and walked over to the bed, climbed up beside Tibbals, sat between her hooves, and put her arms around her.

They sat together for a long time.

Finally, Tibbals spoke. "Preparations have begun for my sire's funeral. We will take him to the catacombs tomorrow. There will be a long procession throughout the city. I would like you to be there."

"Of course."

"And I think you should invite the Duende of your village."

Carling hadn't thought of that but was glad Tibbals had. "Higson and I will go today to invite them."

Tibbals nodded in appreciation.

Two of Tandum's friends agreed to carry Carling and Higson to the village of Duende. The two Duende would never be able to cover the distance from Minsheen to their village and back in one day. Carling was excited to return to her home. So many things had happened in the few weeks she had been gone. She hoped all was well.

As they approached the village of Duenton, the young Duende girl was relieved to see the city wall they had built still standing tall and strong. She waved at the Fauns who were manning the watchtowers. They waved back excitedly.

"Carling and Higson are arriving! Carling and Higson are arriving!" they shouted down to the villagers.

By the time Carling and Higson, riding on the backs of the Centaurs, entered the village, several Duende had gathered in the square to greet them. Carling grinned widely and waved enthusiastically before her Centaur even came to a halt. When her mount did fully stop, she swung her legs over his back and slid to the ground. She was immediately surrounded by the villagers, all of whom were shouting words of welcome at once.

Ashtic, the maker of the Silver Breastplate and her instructor in the art of wielding a sword, stepped up and shook her hand. "We have missed you and worried about you. Is all well?"

"No, Ashtic. I have sad news to report."

Ashtic's expression immediately changed from happiness to sadness as his single bushy eyebrow fell until it nearly hid his eyes and his smile turned to a frown. "What have you come to tell us?"

"Manti has been killed."

A gasp went up from the crowd followed by exclamations of shock and sadness.

"Oh, no!"

"It can't be true!"

"That is so very sad."

"His funeral procession will be held tomorrow," Carling said. "Tibbals—and I believe her family and many other Minsheen Centaurs—would like to have you all there." She looked around at the faces of the Duende whom she knew and loved so well, not surprised when they agreed to attend.

The morning of the funeral was cold and misty. Gray clouds above matched the mood of the mourners who had gathered in the city square to join Manti's funeral procession. The wind blew the black flags that hung from every stable and shop and the black banners that covered the palace windows. To Carling, it seemed as though the very heavens were joining them in expressing their sorrow.

Carling walked to the top step of the government building so she could see over the heads of the Centaurs. Higson was soon by her side. "It's a sad day," he said.

Carling sniffed and wiped at her nose. "It is," she said, her voice cracking.

They didn't have to wait long. Soon a large carriage appeared from around the corner of the government building. It was being pulled by eight burly Centaurs dressed in matching black and gold shirts with long black capes attached at their necks that flowed back over their haunches. Their legs were wrapped with black strips of fabric, and their tails were braided with black ribbon. The carriage transporting Manti's body was covered in gold fabric and surrounded with flowers.

Right behind the carriage, with heads bowed and shoulders rounded, walked Tamah, Tibbals, and Tandum. As they passed, Centaurs fell in step behind them. Carling grabbed Higson's hand and dashed down the steps to join the procession. As they reached the city gates, Carling saw a large group of very tired-looking Duende and several Fauns who had traveled through the night to reach the city of Minsheen to pay their respects. Carling felt her heart swell with gratitude, and she smiled as she motioned for them to join her in the line.

The carriage led them up the sides of Mount Dashmore. The climb was steep and rugged, and Carling realized very quickly why eight Centaurs were needed to pull Manti's body. As the carriage bounced over rocks and ruts, flower petals broke off and fluttered away in the wind that was becoming increasingly strong and cold as they climbed higher and higher.

When the carriage finally came to a stop, it was in front of a large opening to a cave. Carling and Higson worked their way between Centaur legs until they were beside Tibbals and Tandum.

"What is this?" Carling whispered to Tibbals.

"We call this 'The Cave of the Kings.' It is the burial place of all the past lead stallions. It is a great honor to be buried here," Tibbals said.

The eight Centaurs who had been pulling the carriage removed their harnesses. Carling could see the perspiration running down their faces and the effort they were making to suck in enough air to replenish their starving lungs. Several Centaurs lit torches, entered the dark cave, and placed themselves at close range from one another, lighting the path.

"You may come with me," Tibbals whispered. Together Carling and Higson followed Tamah, Tandum, and Tibbals into the cave. They walked silently between the Centaurs who were lighting their way with torches held high above their heads. Carling looked around as the flickering flames cast eerie shadows over the rough walls and ceiling of the large grotto. She felt a shiver go down her spine and reached over and clutched Higson's hand, grateful when he squeezed hers in return.

Tamah stopped in front of a chiseled-out catacomb. On either side of the opening, two more Centaurs stood with long narrow brass horns, called lurs, in their hands. They raised them to their lips and blew into them, releasing a long, mournful sound that echoed throughout the cavern. By changing the arrangement of their facial muscles, they changed the pitch of the sound coming out of the horns. Together, the two Centaurs played a sad but beautiful tune Carling had never heard before.

"The song is called 'Praise to His Soul,'" Tibbals whispered to Carling and Higson. "It is always played at our funerals."

Carling nodded in acknowledgement and let a tear trickle down her cheek.

When the song was over, the two Centaurs lowered their lurs to their sides and stood stiffly. Carling heard the clip-clop sound of numerous hooves on the stone floor of the cave coming from behind her. She turned and watched as a dozen Centaurs approached, carrying Manti. His body was draped in a scarlet and gold burial shroud that sparkled in the firelight.

Tamah let out a high-pitched wail, prompting Tandum and Tibbals to throw their arms around her and bury their faces in her long hair.

The twelve Centaurs bearing Manti's body carried him to the narrow crypt and placed his body inside. Then they stepped out and rolled a large stone in front of the opening, sealing it off completely.

Tamah brushed the tears from her face, turned, and led the way out of the cave. Tandum followed next, then Tibbals. Tibbals's tail drooped so low it was dragging on the ground. Carling watched them go, fearing her heart would break in two. With one last look at the stone that covered Manti's burial place, she, too, left the cave.

CHAPTER 29

Electing a New Leader

THE BLACK FLAGS AND banners continued to flap in the breeze for the next week as a feeling of melancholy continued to hang over the city of Minsheen. Much as Carling wanted to escape and return to her village, she understood why Tibbals begged her to stay. Realizing that her friend needed her, she conceded.

For a full week, Carling dressed each day in a simple black dress. But, at last, the week of mourning was past. Carling arose, set aside her black dress, and instead covered her silver breastplate with a soft, flowing purple dress that just matched her eyes. She pulled her auburn curls away from her face and secured them with ornate silver clips Tibbals had given her. Then she ate a light breakfast and left her room in search of Higson.

Higson, of course, was already up and practicing his bow and arrow skills in the palace courtyard. He, too, had abandoned his mourning attire for his typical brown shirt and pants.

"Good morning, Higson," Carling said. "Will you come with me to the city square? Yesterday Tibbals told me they are going to announce the new leader of Minsheen this morning."

Higson turned and looked at Carling, his mouth dropping open as he lowered his bow and arrow.

"What?" said Carling, cocking her head.

"Um-m-m, well," Higson stammered, his face turning red. "I'd just gotten used to seeing you in black. You look, um-m-m, really nice."

Carling smiled. "Why thank you, Higson. Shall we go?" she said, making a point not to mention the color of his cheeks.

Carling and Higson hurried to the city square. They were far from the first to arrive. Most of the population of Minsheen was already there, waiting in eager anticipation for the decision to be announced. Only a few of the Centaurs carried on their business. The rest were gathered in the city square.

As the sun rose higher in the sky, so did everyone's anxiety. Carling, with Higson right behind, wound her way among the Centaurs, listening to their conversations. When one discussion in particular caught her attention, she stopped to listen.

"I really don't know what's taking them so long," exclaimed one stallion.

"Shouldn't it just go to Zarius?" said a mare. "He's the senior council member, after all."

"I really hope they don't select him," said another stallion.

"Why not?" said someone else.

Carling perked up her pointed ears, eager to hear the response.

The stallion shook his head and lifted his shoulders. "I don't know. I just don't trust him."

"Well, he's no Manti, that's for sure."

"I've heard from his mare he has a terrible temper."

"And he kicks his colts and fillies."

"Tsk, tsk," clucked several mares.

Carling scratched her head and knotted her eyebrows in confusion. She decided to find Tibbals and see what she thought about all of this. "Let's go find Tibbals and Tandum," she said to Higson as she grabbed his hand and pulled him around the Centaur legs that surrounded them.

The future queen went back to the palace. There she found Tibbals and Tandum sitting alone in a parlor. "May we come in?" she asked, peeking around a doorframe.

"Of course," said Tibbals with a smile, her arms extended in welcome.

Carling and Higson walked softly into the room. Carling noticed Tibbals had discarded her black blouse for a yellow one, but Carling could tell by the puffiness around her eyes that she had been crying.

The two Centaurs were seated on beautiful lounges covered in red brocade fabric. The room they occupied was filled with bouquets of flowers, no doubt sent by friends and well-wishers. Those same flowers filled the room with a sweet aroma. Carling breathed in deeply as she walked up to Tibbals, who was patting the couch cushion beside her. "Sit by me, dear Carling." Carling climbed up on the soft couch while Higson sat on the floor in front of them.

"Any news?" Tandum asked.

Carling shook her head. "Not yet. Does it always take this long for the council to decide on a new leader?"

"Well," Tibbals said, "Tandum and I haven't been alive for the selection of a new lead stallion. Our father was the leader all of our lives. However, Mother says it is always quick and orderly."

"I can't understand why it should take so long. It seems Zarius would move into that position," said Tandum.

"What do you think of Zarius?" Carling asked him.

"Well, I don't really know him," he answered.

"I don't think Mother likes him," said Tibbals.

"And I know he and Father didn't see eye to eye on many things," added Tandum.

"Such as what?" asked Carling, eager to understand the dynamics behind the Centaur council and its decisions.

"For one thing, Zarius agreed with our uncle about doing whatever was necessary to secure the throne of Crystonia for the Centaurs," said Tandum.

"Even if that meant bloodshed," added Tibbals. "Father was completely against this. He believed in waiting for the rightful heir...um...*you!*"

"Even if that heir is a little Duende?" whispered Carling.

At that moment, the sounds of hooves echoed outside the parlor. Carling, Higson, Tandum, and Tibbals snapped their heads around in unison just as two Centaurs entered the room.

"A decision has been reached. The council is leaving their chambers and will make an announcement shortly. Come quickly," said one of the Centaurs.

Carling and Higson climbed on the backs of Tibbals and Tandum, who rushed out the door. Even though they had hurried as quickly as possible, they were some of the last to arrive in the city square. Word must have spread like a bad cold, for the square was now filled with Centaurs, their hooves stomping and tails swishing with both impatience and eager anticipation. Everyone wanted to hear for themselves just who would be the new lead stallion.

The doors to the government building opened wide and Adivino walked out, followed by all of the council members. Adivino stopped at the top of the long staircase and gazed over the crowd. He nodded and smiled in acknowledgement of the applause that rippled through the gathering. Then he stood still for a moment, running his fingers through his long white beard. Finally, he held up his hands to silence everyone, his pale blue eyes twinkling.

"Greetings, citizens of Minsheen," he said, looking around. He suddenly caught Carling's eye and added, "and honored guests."

He cleared his throat. "I know you didn't come here to listen to me pontificate." Chuckles sprinkled through the crowd. "So, I will get right to the point. With the passing of our dearly beloved lead stallion, Manti, it became necessary to select a new leader." He motioned to the council members, who were now lined up behind him. "These are your council members, all very qualified Centaurs to be sure. However, it was necessary to select one to lead them and us." He paused and looked directly at Carling. "At least until the rightful heir to the throne of Crystonia is prepared to take over that responsibility."

Murmurs spread through the crowd. "Does he know something we don't?" whispered a stallion behind Carling and Tibbals. Tibbals turned and looked at him but said nothing.

"As I was saying," Adivino continued, "we need a new lead stallion. Therefore, the council has spent many hours in discussion and debate, which, I will admit, was heated at times." Several of the council members cast their gazes skyward. Carling noticed that others turned their heads and looked at Zarius, who was standing off to one side, his arms folded across his chest, his tail swishing. "But, as is always necessary, the council has come to a conclusion. It is my honor to introduce to you your new lead stallion...," he paused for dramatic effect..., "Chauncery."

A loud cheer arose from the crowd, but Carling continued to watch Zarius. The council member's eyes narrowed and his frown deepened, but he didn't move or speak. He simply stood still, glaring at the crowd, his gaze moving from one group of Centaurs to another until he realized Carling was watching him. As his gaze met hers, Zarius raised his eyebrows and gave Carling a sardonic smile that sent chills down her spine.

CHAPTER 30

Betrayal

ZARIUS LISTENED TO THE announcement of the new lead stallion, grinding his teeth, his nails biting into the palms of his hands. The veins on his forehead pulsed. He glared out at the audience as they cheered and applauded Chauncery. *I will show them...all of them,* he thought to himself as he looked over the crowd. Then his eyes alighted upon the little Duende girl. *Can it be true, what Manti told me? Is she, even now, wearing the Silver Breastplate? Is she the one in my way?*

He looked into her eyes and gave her a smile that was really covering a sneer.

As soon as the announcement was complete, the Centaurs gathered around Chauncery to congratulate him. The sight made Zarius sick. The Centaur turned and retreated into the isolation provided by the empty government building. He moved quickly into the council chambers to be alone and think.

Zarius stomped all four hooves as he entered the room he had been in so many times before. He slammed the door behind him, catching his tail hairs in it. With a growl and a yank, he freed his tail and clomped into the room and up to the front, where the council members' chairs sat neatly tucked up to their desks. He turned back to face the room. "This should have been mine!" he yelled at the empty room. "I had the right to rule. *I* am the senior council member!" His anger burst forth in a blast of kicks from his hind legs that sent chairs flying. Taking deep breaths, he grabbed a table and threw it at a window. With a loud crash, the glass burst out and fell to the ground, leaving a gaping hole in what had once been a beautiful stained-glass window.

Zarius turned to the next table and grabbed it, lifting it in the air.

"I think it would be best if you put that down."

Zarius spun around, the table still in the air above his head. Adivino was standing just inside the door.

"What are you doing here?" asked Zarius, his words filled with scorn, his lips curling over his teeth in disgust.

"Looking for you," said Adivino calmly. "And it appears I found you just in time...at least before you could do any more damage."

Zarius dropped the table, causing a leg to break when it hit the stone floor. "Ha," he said with disgust as he kicked the table.

Adivino limped up to Zarius. His age and arthritis were slowing him down these days. "Zarius, I understand why you are upset."

"Do you?" Zarius responded as he turned his back on the herd historian.

"Yes, I do. In fact, I was in your position once."

This caught Zarius's attention, but he refused to show it and kept his back to Adivino.

"There was a time when I, too, was the senior council member. I was passed over for the job of lead stallion when another was selected in my place. A much finer and younger stallion, I might add. His name was Manti. It took me a long time to come to grips with the fact that another had been chosen over me. But gradually I became aware of my real talents and what I could contribute to the herd." Adivino paused and walked around to face Zarius.

"You, Zarius, are a Centaur of many talents as well. You can be very helpful to the Minsheen herd and the new lead stallion if you so choose. Are you going to let this disappointment destroy you? Or are you going to use it to make you stronger and better? The choice is yours."

Zarius narrowed his eyes. "Perhaps our definition of stronger and better is different, old stallion."

Zarius cantered through the Forest of Rumors, working his way between trees and brush, always moving in a northerly direction. He had never been to Fort Heilodius, but he knew the general location on the slopes of Mount Heilodius. The oppressive darkness of the forest pressed down on him, but he refused to let himself be deterred. His internal compass kept him going in the right direction. By the time the sun whispered that it would soon be up, he could see the fortress walls.

Zarius approached the heavy iron gate of the fort with some degree of trepidation. He felt the perspiration on his torso soaking his shirt and the sweat running down his face, stinging his eyes. He didn't know if it was from the exertion of cantering most of the night through the forest or from the anxiety he was now feeling. He realized, for the first time, that he hadn't really thought this through completely. He wasn't sure what he was going to say to the Commander. Coming here had been an impulsive action born of a desire for revenge. Not that he was now doubting his decision—in his mind it was his only option. But he hadn't yet figured out just what he wanted and how to go about getting it.

As he reached the gate he heard a guard yell at him. "Who goes there?"

Zarius looked up at the guard, who was peering down from the tower. "It is Zarius from the city of Minsheen."

"State your business."

"I come seeking an audience with the Commander."

Zarius heard several guards laughing. "What makes you think he'll see you?" said one.

"I can only request that he consent to meeting me. Perhaps it would help if you told him I have information for him regarding the new lead stallion of the Minsheen herd."

Zarius listened and waited as the guard's muffled voices debated back and forth. Finally, the sound of chains creaking and clanging was heard and the heavy iron gate was slowly raised.

"Come in before I change my mind," said the guard who had been the first to speak.

The angry, rebellious, turncoat Centaur stepped through the open gate. He paused momentarily to survey his surroundings. He noticed, right away, the same things Carling had noticed nearly a year earlier: the ramshackle appearance of the hastily constructed buildings, the unkempt courtyard littered with trash and manure, the sullen looks on the faces of the fort's inhabitants, especially the mares. He lifted his nose in haughtiness and turned to one of the guards. "Where might I find the Commander?"

"Follow me. I will lead you there."

The guard led Zarius up the hill, weaving through narrow alleyways. "Why are you taking me through the back streets?" queried the Commander, suspicious of everything around him.

The guard stopped and turned to face him. "*Back* streets? You're not in the city of Minsheen anymore. This is the only way to go."

"Alright, then. Carry on, carry on," said Zarius with a wave of his hand.

They finally stopped in front of the only substantial-looking building in the fort. A large fortress made of irregular-shaped stones in shades of gray and brown with a gray slate roof loomed in front of them. Side by side, the two Centaurs, one in a black soldier's uniform and one in the red shirt worn by the elite of the Minsheen herd, walked up the steps, carefully placing each hoof.

The guard rapped on the rough wooden door. Someone slid open a small panel in the center of the door, and Zarius found himself looking into a dark brown eye. Immediately an eyelid hooded the eye. "What do you want?" a voice said.

"This Centaur has come to meet with the Commander."

The eye shifted and stared at the guard. "So? So does everyone."

"He says he has important information about the new lead stallion of the Minsheen herd."

"Oh, he does, does he?" The eye rolled back to look at Zarius. "Just what makes you think the Commander cares?"

"Oh, he cares, alright," said Zarius, lifting his chin and stomping one hoof. He was getting tired of trying to be polite. His patience was spent. "I insist that you admit me at once. I must speak to the Commander."

"Well, you don't have to get all huffy about it!" said the voice.

So that's how these deplorable peons need to be talked to, is it? No problem there. I can handle that, thought Zarius, a smile on his face born of a firm belief in his own superiority. He felt his heart rate rising.

Once the door was opened, Zarius entered. He gave the guard inside a dismissive nod and said, "You will learn to not stand in my way again."

The guard saluted and stepped back.

Zarius continued forward to the next guard. "Take me to the Commander."

The Commander had not been seen out of his quarters since the night he returned to the fort covered in his own blood. When Zarius entered his darkened room, he could see why. The Commander lay on his bed, bandages wrapped tightly around his chest. His face was pale; his hair was soaked in sweat and matted in dark curls against his forehead. When Zarius approached the bed, he saw the Commander's eyes were closed and his breathing was shallow and raspy.

Hum-m-m, thought Zarius as he stood beside the bed, looking down at this once bold and brave leader, *this changes everything.*

Zarius reached down and shook the Commander's shoulder.

Snort. Groan. The Commander slowly opened his eyes. As soon as he focused on his visitor, he started. "What are you doing here, Zarius?" he said in a weak, groggy voice, his eyes narrowed with suspicion. "Have you come seeking revenge?"

"I have come to let you know a new lead stallion of the Minsheen herd has been selected."

"Is it you?"

"No. If it were me, do you think I would be here?"

"No, I guess you wouldn't." The Commander attempted to take a deep breath but began coughing violently. He squeezed his eyes shut and did his best to get the coughing under control. Finally, he spoke again. "I think I'm beginning to understand your motive for being here," he said, "but I will let *you* tell me who the new lead stallion is and why you have *really* come." The Commander seemed to be getting weaker with each breath he took and each word he was able to force out.

"The new lead stallion is Chauncery."

The Commander slowly opened his eyes and nodded. "Another Manti, then. They are following the same foolish course. But tell me. Why were you not selected? You were the senior council member and therefore should have been moved into that position." His voice was reduced to a whisper. Clearly the effort it took just to speak was too much for him.

Zarius stood and began pacing. "You're right," he said with a growl. "I should be the lead stallion."

"So that is why you are here." Getting weaker by the minute, the Commander closed his eyes again.

"Yes."

"What do you want from me?"

Zarius stopped pacing. "I want to be the head of the Heilodius herd. I want your blessing before you die."

"Who said I am going to die?" the Commander demanded as forcefully as he could, his face turning red, the veins on his forehead pulsing. "Who said I need a replacement?"

"No one said anything. But just look at you. It's obvious the end is even now upon you. You need to name your successor before you die. I want you to name me."

"Why should I?"

"Because you and I think alike. I will carry on your mission to secure the throne for the Centaurs."

"Do you not know about the Duende girl?"

Zarius looked up at the ceiling as he considered his response. Then he lowered his gaze and looked at the Commander. "Manti told me the Silver Breastplate had appeared. It was his intent to honor the girl and support her. That is not my intent...like you, I might add."

The Commander smiled weakly. "You are very wise, Zarius. I will take your request into consideration." He took a deep breath as though it took all his might to speak. "But the girl needs to be removed from the equation," he finally added. "Do you have the conviction to do that?"

"Absolutely," Zarius said. "It would be a pleasure."

CHAPTER 31

A New Commander

THE NEXT MORNING THE Commander was weaker than ever, barely clinging to life. His breathing was shallow. He lay in his bed and moaned. Zarius lounged on a chair beside him, not that he was the attentive nurse or friend. He just wanted to be there when the Commander took his last breath to make sure it happened. Mares came in and out of the room to try to provide comfort.

Suddenly, an idea came to him. "Miss, wait right there," he said just as a mare began to leave the room. He shook the Commander roughly. "Commander, Commander, wake up."

The Commander groaned.

"Commander, I want you to confer the leadership upon me in front of a witness."

"Huh?" the Commander mumbled.

Zarius leaned over the Commander and repeated his demand. "The leadership of the Heilodius herd. I want you to designate me as your replacement while we have a witness."

The Commander mumbled something that no one in the room could understand.

Zarius stood upright as a big smile spread across his face. Turning toward the mare, he said, "See? He just said I'm supposed to take his place as Commander. He said it as plain as day. You heard it, didn't you?"

The mare cocked her head and, a confused look on her face, said, "I...I...I guess I did."

"Yes! Right, you did!" Zarius rushed over to her and escorted her out the door. "Now go tell everyone you see what you just heard. Hurry!"

Zarius turned back into the room, a terrible grin now twisting his face. He stepped over to the wardrobe and threw open the doors. Hanging in the cupboard were a dozen identical shirts–black with a silver crown surround by silver stars across the front–the Commander's shirts. Zarius pulled one off a wooden hanger and held it up, admiring its beauty. In fact, he didn't think he had ever seen anything so beautiful. It took him only a minute to remove his red shirt and replace it with the black one.

Just as he was admiring himself in a mirror, he heard the Commander groan and thrash in his bed. Zarius stopped his primping as a rush of adrenaline filled him with strength. He moved slowly and deliberately toward the bed. Reaching forth his hands, he made sure the Commander would never groan again.

Dressed in his new uniform, which he'd stolen from the Commander's own closet, Zarius stepped out of the fortress and made his way down the winding alleyways to the large courtyard just inside the gates. The Heilodius army was running through their morning drills but stopped abruptly when they saw him approach. They saluted this new Centaur dressed in the uniform of the Commander.

Zarius suddenly felt taller, bigger, stronger. The feeling that he could conquer the world flowed through him. He breathed in several deep and satisfied breaths, thrust out his chest, and smiled at his army.

Extending his arms, he said, "My revered, respected and...yes...*feared* army." A cheer went up from the soldiers. Zarius's smile widened and a feeling of deep satisfaction filled him with warmth.

He raised his palms to quiet the crowd. He looked from side to side. *This is where I belong*, he said to himself before continuing. "It is with deep sorrow that I announce the passing of your beloved Commander. It is with great humility that I take the position of his successor that he so generously conferred upon me with his last dying breaths. Oh, that I wish he had not bequeathed this role to me, for the burden of such a responsibility weighs heavily upon me from my head to my haunches." He swished his tail to illustrate the point.

"But we have much to do to carry on his work and achieve his dream of Centaur dominance in the land of Crystonia." Another cheer went up from the army.

Zarius raised his hands again and nodded. "Yes, yes. I, too, carry in my heart the same enthusiasm for our mission. However, there is a job we must complete first."

A hush went over the crowd. Zarius smiled. *I have them in the palm of my hand and the sole of my hoof.* "There is one who is responsible for the murder of our beloved Commander. This one is, even now, being sheltered by our enemies in the city of Minsheen. We must go to that city and retrieve this one. Reparation must be paid for the vile act of killing our leader. This one is a young Duende girl by the name of Carling."

CHAPTER 32

Warning

BALE AND DALT WERE manning the two guard towers on either side of the large iron gate, which was currently in the down position. They listened to Zarius, their new Commander, as he made his speech. As soon as they heard Carling's name, they looked at one another. Their eyes met, and they both understood the silent communication that passed between them.

As though choreographed ahead of time, both Centaurs whirled around and dashed down the tower stairs. They met at the bottom in front of the gate.

"What should we do?" asked Dalt.

"We need to warn Carling," replied Bale.

"Okay. Let's get going," said Dalt. "Let's use the back gate so no one will see us."

The back gate was the same door through which they had helped Carling, Higson, Tibbals, and Tandum escape from prison several months earlier. At that time, Carling only had the Stone of Mercy. Now she was one stone closer to inheriting the throne and her life was in danger. They knew they needed to help her again.

Bale and Dalt dashed to the stone fortress and entered the front doors. They rushed through the main foyer to the little door far in the back of the building. They knew this door would lead them out of Fort Heilodius.

Only Adivino and the council members were aware of Zarius's disappearance. Carling and Higson were caught up in the excitement that had replaced the mourning. They paid no attention to Zarius's absence at the banquets and other celebrations going on throughout the city as the new leader was welcomed to his post. The black banners that once hung from the windows and doorways were now replaced with garlands of flowers. Everywhere, the city was filled with laughter and music, singing and dancing...and delicious food!

"Oh, Higson, try this," exclaimed Carling, passing a frosting-covered pastry across the table in the town square at which they were seated.

Higson took it eagerly, never one to pass up something to eat, especially if it was sweet. He took a bite. His eyes closed and a smile spread across his face as the sweet delicacy melted in his mouth. The rest of the pastry disappeared quickly. "I need another one!" he said while wiping frosting from his chin.

Carling laughed with delight.

"Try some of these," offered Tibbals, passing a dish filled with sugared berries.

Tandum plopped down on a bench beside them. He gasped for breath and wiped sweat off his forehead.

"What's the matter?" asked Tibbals.

"If one more filly asks me to dance, I swear I will die!"

Carling, Higson, and Tibbals erupted in laughter.

"Oh, you poor, poor colt. Such a problem to have," sighed Tibbals in mock sympathy.

Carling smiled as she looked at Tandum and Tibbals lovingly bantering back and forth. She felt a lightness in her chest and a warmth that spread through her body. For a brief time, she was able to forget the burden she carried and just enjoy the celebrations. She felt a welcome satisfaction and contentment.

It would be short lived.

The parties continued on into the night. Lanterns hanging from the trees set off a warm glow. The feasting continued as well. Carling was warm and full, both sensations making her sleepy. She and Higson had long since ceased dancing and were happy to just sit under the lanterns and watch the festivities. Higson placed his arm around her and she leaned against his shoulder. She was soon lost to her dreams...happy ones.

Carling was jolted awake by the shaking. "Carling. Carling, wake up." It was Higson.

Carling wiggled and stretched, then rubbed her violet eyes. She brushed her auburn curls out of her face. "What is it?" she asked. The contented smile that had covered her face melted as soon as she saw the worried looks on the faces around her. Higson still sat beside her, propping her up. In front of her stood Adivino, Tibbals, Tandum, and, to her surprise, Bale and Dalt.

"What is it? What's the matter?" she stammered.

Adivino bent down and took her hands. "My dear, your friends, Bale and Dalt, have come from Fort Heilodius with some very disturbing news."

Carling looked over at Bale and Dalt, noticing just now their heavy breathing and sweat-soaked clothing. She felt her heart start to pound. "What is the news? Tell me."

Adivino looked softly into her eyes. "Bale and Dalt have come to give you a warning. I will let them tell you." He let go of her hands and stepped back, giving Bale and Dalt a nod of encouragement.

"Carling, the Commander is dead," said Bale.

Carling gasped. Tears immediately filled her eyes and spilled down her cheeks. "Oh, no-o-o-o! I killed him. I killed him," she moaned.

Tibbals pushed past Bale and Dalt and wrapped her arms around the young Duende. "You did what you had to do. You were trying to save my father."

Carling shuddered and stiffened. "I never wanted any of this."

Higson turned her chin so she faced him. "But Crystonia needs you."

"Not me."

"Yes, you," Higson said firmly.

Dalt interjected. "That isn't all we have to tell you."

Carling looked up at him. She bit her lip and nodded, encouraging him to continue.

Dalt cleared his throat and wiped his forehead with the back of his black sleeve. "Zarius has been appointed as the new Commander."

An audible gasp was heard coming from everyone. "Z-Z-Zarius?" Tibbals stammered, her wide eyes showing her shock.

"That traitor," sneered Tandum through clenched teeth.

"Why would Zarius do such a thing?" asked Carling.

"His heart is filled with pride," said Adivino. "When the council rejected him for the position of lead stallion, he was terribly angry. He must have decided this was the best way to get back at the Minsheen herd. I must say, I'm not surprised."

"I see," said Carling.

"But that is not all," said Bale.

Carling looked at him and cocked her head. "What else do you need to tell us?"

"Zarius is preparing to come with a band of soldiers to Minsheen to capture *you!*"

CHAPTER 33

Seeking Safety

EVERYONE WAS SILENT FOR a moment as they considered this new information.

Adivino spoke first. "Carling, I think you should leave the city of Minsheen and find a safe place to hide."

"I agree," said Higson.

"As do I," said Tibbals.

Carling looked back and forth, trying to read their expressions. Some looked worried, others looked angry. She wasn't sure how she felt. "How much time do I have before they get to the city?" she asked Bale and Dalt.

"They were assembling the band when we left early yesterday morning. It is our guess that they will set out by tomorrow morning," said Dalt.

"Then I should leave before the morning. I should leave right now," Carling said, brushing her hair out of her eyes. "I will go and get prepared."

Carling went to her room and found her bag. She began gathering her few belongs and putting them into her bag. As she did so, her mind was racing. She kept asking herself the same question over and over. *Where should I go? Where should I go?*

"Such a pity. Such a pity."

Carling spun around. "Hello, Shim."

"On the run again, I see," he said as he sat cross-legged on her bed.

Carling sighed and went back to stuffing things into her little bag.

"So where to this time?" Shim said, resting his chin on his fists and raising his eyebrows.

"I don't know. Do you have any suggestions?" she said, turning to face the Tommy Knocker.

Shim sat up and scratched the bristles on his chin. "As a matter of fact, I do. I will hide my jewel...er...I mean, *you*, in the Cave of the Bats."

Shim's slip of the tongue was not lost on Carling, but she considered the offer anyway. "Hum-m-m. That would be a good hiding place. I'm quite sure Zarius would never find me there." She scratched her head.

There was a tap on the door. "Come in," said Carling.

Higson entered the room. "Are you ready to go?"

"Yes. Shim suggested that we go to his cave."

"Shim?" said Higson, looking around the room.

Carling looked back at the spot on her bed where Shim had been sitting just a moment before. "Okay, Shim. It's only Higson. You can show yourself."

A popping sound was heard and Shim reappeared on the far side of the room, peeking around the window drapes.

"Shim, I hate the way you do that," said Carling, only half teasing.

"It's my best talent," said Shim as he stepped out from behind the curtains.

Higson's face showed his disdain for the Tommy Knocker as he considered this option. "Well, I guess that would be alright," he finally said. "Are you going to lead us?" he asked Shim.

"Do I look like a tour guide? I generously offered my cave, but you'll have to find it yourself. You did it before. I don't doubt you can do it again." With that, Shim raised his cane, spun around, and disappeared in a twinkle of lights.

Carling and Higson looked at each other. "Do you think we *can* find it again?" asked Carling.

"If we find the Ice Horses, we can. But it's a long, two- or three-day journey, and we will need to avoid the band of Heilodius Centaurs that will be traveling toward Minsheen. I think it might be wiser to hide in Manyon Canyon."

Manyon Canyon was the home of Baskus the eagle, who had been the caretaker of the Stone of Mercy before Carling was sent to retrieve it. The canyon was a full three-day journey from Minsheen but in a southwesterly direction. This would take them away from Zarius and his band. In addition, Carling could count on Baskus to help her. "That might be a good idea. Let's go ask Tibbals and Tandum."

After much discussion, the four friends decided to head southwest through the Forest of Rumors and across the Echoing Plains to the mouth of Manyon Canyon. They hoped they would be able to find shelter in the canyon. The fear of running right into Zarius and his band convinced them to go in the opposite direction from Fort Heilodius and away from the Cave of the Bats.

Carling and Tibbals covered their heads with the cowls of their cloaks and started off in the lead. As they walked through the village, the remains of the festivities made Carling feel a bit melancholy. Just a short time before, she had enjoyed herself with the Centaurs. Now all was quiet. The lanterns hung dark and still. The tables sat askew, scattered with dirty dishes. The dance floor was empty. Memories of the music and laughter seemed to have floated away into the starry night.

They went out the gates and headed south, their trail lit by the full moon. Knowing that Zarius would be approaching from the opposite direction, they didn't worry about stumbling into him. Nor did they feel they needed to rush. Instead, Tibbals and Tandum carried their two Duende riders at a leisurely pace as they entered the dark and foreboding Forest of Rumors. The gentle rocking motion of Tibbals's gait soothed Carling, and soon she nestled up against her friend's back and fell asleep. Higson followed suit and was quickly snoring softly.

The Centaurs moved along steadily, weaving in and out of the thick trees and brush. The trunks of the trees were black and coarse, lined by age and weather. The pine needles and leaves hanging from the intertwined branches were equally dark. They snatched at Tibbals's cape and hood and got tangled in her hair. The forest's sounds from owls as well as animals that howled and growled kept both Tibbals and Tandum on edge.

"I hate this forest," whispered Tibbals as she untangled her long hair from the clutches of a grabby branch. "Especially at night. If I were asleep, I would think I was having a nightmare."

"When Father and I came hunting here, it didn't seem so bad. I guess it was because I was with him," responded Tandum.

A scream, from somewhere to their right, left both Centaurs quivering. "W-what was that?" said Tibbals, quietly so as not to awaken Carling.

"Probably just a raptor," said Tandum, his face pale and his eyes open wide.

The screams carried on periodically throughout the night. Tibbals walked on the toes of her hooves. Tandum kept looking frantically from side to side.

A few hours later, the sun painted the western sky pink. But little light could work its way through the thick canopy overhead. No birds were heard calling to the new day. No squirrels chattered in the trees. Fortunately, the eerie sounds of the night had ceased. The only noises came from the crackling of broken branches under the Centaurs' hooves and from Tibbals and Tandum, who were panting heavily.

A little stream meandered through the forest, its waters dark and cold. Tibbals and Tandum stopped for a drink and a much-needed rest. Once the rocking stopped, Carling and Higson woke up.

"Where are we?" asked Carling with a yawn.

"Somewhere in the Forest of Rumors. I'm trying to get us to the hunting lodge where we stayed on our way back from Manyon Canyon last year," said Tandum.

Carling's mind flashed back to the night in the cabin with the Fauns and the Heilodius Centaurs while a vicious storm raged outside. It was there that she first met Bale and Dalt. Her actions saving both their lives had secured a loyalty that resulted in the warning she had received just the night before.

"I hope it's still there. I sure could use some beauty sleep," said Tibbals as she stretched her arms and rolled her shoulders.

Carling jumped off her back. "I'll walk the rest of the way," she offered.

Higson joined her on the ground. "I will, too."

"You'd better ride," said Tandum. "I don't know where the cabin is from here. It was so dark, we could have spent the entire night walking around in circles for all I know."

Carling reached up and patted the shoulder of his horse body. "It won't hurt us to walk," she said with a sympathetic smile.

They continued resting for quite a while as the sun rose in the sky, its rays trying to worm their way into the darkness of the forest. They ate some rolls and cheese and drank from the cold stream. "When we reach the cabin," said Higson, "I'll go hunting for dinner."

The travelers started working their way between the branches of the trees that grabbed at them as they passed. They moved in the general direction toward where Tandum believed the cabin to be. After several exhausting hours and no sign of the cabin, Tibbals said, "I'm done for today, big brother. My hooves can't take it anymore."

Carling, who had been stumbling along right behind her, came up to her side. "Let's stop here for the night. There are only a couple of hours of daylight left, and Higson needs some hunting time. I'm sure we're far enough away from Zarius to be safe for the time being."

Tandum didn't argue. Instead he began gathering sticks and dry moss to build a fire. Tibbals found a soft bed at the base of a tree, folded her long legs beneath her horse-like body, and leaned her human-like torso against the trunk of the tree. She was soon fast asleep.

Tibbals continued to sleep during their dinner of roasted squirrel, resisting Carling's attempts to awaken her.

"Perhaps we should stay here all night and move on in the morning," Carling said, feeling sorry for Tibbals. "I'm not sure Tibbals could make it another step."

"True that," responded Tandum, no doubt just as tired.

So, as the sun cast its last shadows through the already unnerving forest, darkness crawled over them.

CHAPTER 34

A Visit from the Wizard

HOW LONG CARLING HAD been asleep, she could not have said. Suffice it to say that the waning moon was high overhead, but providing no light, when Carling was awakened by a warm breeze covering her like a soft blanket.

"Carling. Carling, wake up."

Carling opened her eyes. Even in the darkness, she could clearly make out the shape and features of the Wizard of Crystonia. He stood in front of her, glowing like an apparition. His cloak flowed gently in the breeze, making it appear that he was floating above the ground. Perhaps he was; Carling couldn't tell.

"Wizard."

"Carling, what are you doing here?"

"I'm trying to get away from Zarius. He is coming after me with a band of Heilodius Centaurs to...."

"To what?"

For the first time, she realized she didn't know what Zarius planned to do. "I don't know, actually. I guess he wants to capture me."

"But you have the Stone of Courage. Are you afraid of him? Think. Are you afraid of him?"

Carling's hand went to the breastplate and covered the red Stone of Courage. It felt warm to the touch. The squirrel she had eaten for dinner felt like it was alive and crawling around in her stomach. She stared at the Wizard. "Yes. I *am* afraid of him."

"Carling, the Stone of Courage gives you great power if you will learn to use it. Courage is one of the most important traits a great leader can possess, but it is not the absence of fear. Courage is conquering that fear for the sake of always doing what is right. In your life as the queen, you will have many experiences that challenge you. You must have the courage to stand up to those challenges whether they come from your enemies or, harder still, your friends. Running from them will never make you the leader you must become for the sake of Crystonia."

"So I must go back?" she asked sheepishly.

"Yes. You must go back and face Zarius's challenge, whatever it may be."

CHAPTER 35

Facing Zarius

CARLING DIDN'T SLEEP THE rest of the night. She sat on the ground, her legs pulled up to her chest, her arms wrapped tightly around her knees. She rested her chin on her knees and tried to block out the strange sounds all around her and ignore the shivers that crawled up and down her spine. She was filled with relief when Tandum woke up and smiled at her.

"Couldn't sleep?" he asked.

"Not much." She wasn't sure just how to tell Tandum so she decided to just be direct. "Tandum, the Wizard came last night."

Tandum cocked his head and raised his eyebrows, inviting her to continue.

"He told me I need to go back and face Zarius."

Tandum started. "What? Are you sure? Maybe you were just dreaming."

Carling shook her head. "No. It was the Wizard. I need to go back and face Zarius. I can't be the queen if I run and hide from every challenge."

Higson had awakened just in time to hear the conversation. "Carling, do you know what you're saying? You're putting yourself in grave danger."

"I know that I am supposed to prepare to become the queen and I need to start acting like one."

"But you can't be the queen if you're dead!" Higson said, his voice cracking with emotion.

Carling moved over to Higson and hugged him. "I appreciate your concern more than you will ever know. But I won't die. I'm wearing the Silver Breastplate."

The four friends covered the distance back to Minsheen much more quickly than they had coming away. They were rested and traveling in the daylight. The Forest of Rumors seemed to leave them alone as though it knew they were departing. "Go away and don't come back," it seemed to be saying as the branches of the tangled trees pushed them on.

The weary travelers arrived at the Gates of Minsheen just as the sun was casting its final rays against the sparkling white city walls. They realized right away something was wrong. Marching back and forth in front of the half-open gates were two Heilodius Centaurs, spears in hand.

Tibbals and Tandum stopped at the edge of the forest, concealing themselves behind the thick wall of trees. "What should we do?" whispered Tibbals.

"Wait right here," said Carling as she lowered herself to the ground. "I'll go talk to them."

"I'm coming with you," said Higson, his tone of voice leaving no room for argument.

The two Duende walked the short distance to the castle. The Centaur guards stopped pacing and watched them approach.

"What is going on here?" asked Carling, her voice bold and even.

"Well, well, well. The little Duende has returned," said one.

"We've been waiting for you," said another with a sneer. "If you'll be so good as to follow us to the government building, there won't be any trouble."

"Why are we going there?" asked Higson.

The two Centaurs looked at him as though noticing Carling's companion for the first time. "Our new Commander is waiting for this young Duende girl in the council chambers."

"Then we wouldn't want to keep him waiting," said Carling, setting her jaw and looking ahead.

Carling took the lead and headed straight to the government building in the center of the city. As she walked, she hoped the twists and turns she could feel in her stomach weren't visible to those around her. Her mind was a swirl of emotions. The fear was definitely there, but she kept recalling the Wizard's words and tried to conquer her fear with the power provided by the Stone of Courage. She placed her hand over the stone on the breastplate and kept walking, placing one foot ahead of the other.

What will I say? What will I do? she kept asking herself. *Are all queens this unsure of themselves?*

Carling walked up the long staircase that led to the doors of the government building. Higson kept up with her. Just before she reached the doors, he grabbed her arm and stopped her. "What are you going to do?" he said.

"I don't know yet."

He raised his eyebrows in concern. "Do you want to stay out here for a bit until you figure it out?"

Carling shook her head. "No. I'll figure it out as I go."

With Higson by her side, Carling walked across the large atrium and into the council chambers. She didn't wait to be announced. Upon her arrival, the discussions that were going on between the numerous Heilodius soldiers in the room ceased and silence filled the room. Every head turned in her direction. Every eye was upon her.

Carling took a quick scan of the situation. Zarius was seated in Manti's old chair. Carling looked for Chauncery and finally found him restrained with ropes between two Heilodius Centaurs. Zarius's soldiers were stationed all around the room, each guarding a bound Council member.

Carling walked boldly up to the front of the room and stood before Zarius.

"Well, well, well, the queen has returned," he said with a chuckle. "I thought that, perhaps, you had abandoned your kingdom and your subjects for your own safety."

"Zarius, what is the meaning of all this?" Carling asked, the sweep of her hand indicting she was referring to the apparent take-over of the council.

"I have decided I like Minsheen better than Fort Heilodius," Zarius said, a crooked smile spreading across his face.

"Zarius, you need to leave," said Carling, staring him straight in the eyes.

Not swayed by the intensity of her violet eyes, he stood and pulled a sword from its sheath. "Make me."

A gasp was heard throughout the room. One of Zarius's soldiers leaned over and said, "You can't fight an unarmed little girl."

"Give her a sword, then," he said, still keeping his eyes locked on hers.

Someone handed Carling a sword. She took it robotically, barely cognizant of the cold steel and heavy weight in her hand.

"Carling, no!" shouted Higson.

Her friend's voice seemed to pull her out of her near trance and she looked down at the sword she was holding. Suddenly, a lightness filled her and she tossed her auburn curls out of her face. She stood up straighter, threw her shoulders back, and raised her sword in a defensive position.

Zarius leaped from the podium, landing squarely on all four hooves right in front of the little Duende. The Centaurs all around the room backed up. Higson stepped in front of Carling, his arms spread wide.

"Higson, I've got this," said Carling with cool confidence. "Get out of the way,"

Tentatively, Higson moved to one side, perspiration pouring down his face, his hands shaking.

Carling displayed none of those signs of apprehension. Instead, she stood her ground and kept her eyes on Zarius.

A roar broke from the Centaur's lips and he charged, his sword held high in the air above his head, his face twisted with anger.

Carling lifted her sword high over her head, blocking Zarius's downward slice. She spun around and her sword clashed with her opponent's, shaking the room with the clash of metal against metal. Carling pulled away, trying desperately to remember all the instructions Ashtic had given her. She knew she could not beat Zarius with strength, but perhaps speed and her small size would give her an advantage. Ashtic always stressed precision, precision, precision. *Where would the best place to attack be? I don't want to kill him. I just want to injure him...and not get injured myself,* she thought.

Carling dashed under Zarius's belly. The Centaur bent down to find her, growling as he did so. She ran around behind him, grabbing his long tail, which he swished. This proved only to propel her further and faster to one side. The new Commander reared up on his hind legs, spinning as he did so. He came down with a loud clang as his front hooves struck the floor of the council chambers, sending sparks in all directions. Zarius glared at Carling and snarled. He swung his sword across the middle of her torso as if to slice her in half. The force of it sent her to the ground, but the Silver Breastplate more than just protected her. It sent a shockwave back up Zarius's sword and though his arm to his body. He yelled several Centaur curse words and stepped back, rubbing his arm.

Carling scrambled to her feet and sucked in several deep breaths, keeping her violet eyes on her opponent. Zarius lunged toward her, his arm outstretched. She dodged his sword easily and swung her own sword over and down across his arm. He jumped back with a yelp, clutching his arm to his chest with his other hand. Blood ran down his sword from the wound and dripped onto the stone floor. He glared at Carling, his teeth clenched in both anger and pain.

Duly shamed, Zarius started to canter toward the chamber door. Just before leaving the room, however, he stopped and looked back at Carling, hatred radiating from his eyes. "This will not be the end, young Duende. We will meet on the field of battle again."

To be continued...

The Centaur Chronicles
Book 3
The Stone of Integrity

ABOUT THE AUTHOR

Winner of numerous literary awards for her middle-grade and young adult fantasies and novels, M.J. Evans loves to incorporate her love of horses into her stories. An avid equestrian from childhood, M.J. Evans enjoys competing in dressage and riding the trails that weave through the colorful Colorado mountains.

Her husband, children and grandchildren are the jewels in her Silver Breastplate.

Contact M.J. Evans on her website:
www.mjevansbooks.com
or
www.dancinghorsepress.com

Additional Titles by M.J. Evans

The Mist Trilogy:
Mom's Choice Award Gold Medal Winner
Behind the Mist
Mists of Darkness
The Rising Mist

North Mystic
First Place winner of the Purple Dragonfly Award
Finalist in the Colorado Authors' League Awards

In the Heart of a Mustang
Gold Medal Winner of the Literary Classics Award
Literary Classics Seal of Approval
Nautilus Book Award Silver Medal

The Centaur Chronicles
Book 1-The Stone of Mercy
Gold Medal winner of the Feathered Quill Award

"Like" these books on Facebook:
Behind the Mist
North Mystic
In the Heart of a Mustang

Follow the author's blog about famous horses
and anything else horse related:
www.themisttrilogy.blogspot.com

The author loves to receive letters from her readers and always writes back: Find her email on her website: www.dancinghorsepress.com

CPSIA information can be obtained
at www.ICGtesting.com
Printed in the USA
LVOW03s1922170118
563091LV00001B/136/P